# SHE
# TORMENTED

ONE MIND. SEVEN HOSTS.

First published in the United Kingdom in 2022
by Daniel J Knight Publishing and Amazon KDP

Paperback ISBN 979 8 436 73352 4
eBook ASIN B09WJ21GVF

Daniel J Knight Publishing
United Kingdom

*You know you read that book*
*But you can't remember reading it*
*You know you drove that journey*
*But you can't remember steering it*
*You know you ordered food today*
*But you can't remember eating it*

*I know I saw another day*
*But I can't remember living it*

BY

DANIEL J KNIGHT

For June,
A mother's love carries a lifetime full.
You are the reason I became, and the reason I am.
This is my gift to you.
To the stars, you now call home.

# PROLOGUE

Five Years Ago.

A s the two sat awkwardly at opposing ends of the small, scratched metal table, Doctor Perkins asked Rhian, "Do you remember what happens here? What this room is?"

Of course, she did. As she glanced upon his white coat, she remembered the years she'd been in and out of that seat in the quest for peace. She'd occupied the same, white-walled claustrophobic room umpteen times in her search for answers and silent prayers for help. Familiar was the ceiling and the air conditioning unit that blew directly down upon her in an isolated wind. It fluttered the single wisp of chestnut hair that dropped over her eye, separated from the wavy locks that sat upon her shoulders. She hesitated; a silent prayer that maybe this time something would go right.

"I do," she said, with a soft nod. "You -- you will tell me who comes out won't you?"

"Of course, as I always do." He was right, he had never lied to Rhian. It was why she trusted him. A smile cracked while his lips remained shut, which provided her with the comfort she needed in the tense moment.

Doctor Perkins neatened the thin pile of creased documents scattered in front of him. It was almost like he'd thrown them there. He scrunched his face and itched his thick-rimmed glasses back into place on the bridge of his crooked nose. He took the time to reach out to his patient one last time. A thoughtful, composed man who knew exactly what he was doing.

"On whose terms?"

"Mine," she replied. A hint of doubt cast over her like a shadow.

"Perfect. Now, remember, if today, tomorrow... whenever, you feel like maybe you don't want to do this then you tell me. We'll just take a break instead, how does that sound?"

As she tucked her hair behind her cold, stiff ears, Rhian straightened her back and lugged the chair closer with a scrape that yelped as it scored the tiled floor. She locked her hands between her legs, under the table. The pupils of her ocean blue eyes bounced off every surface in the room, scarce as they were, and then locked on the mature man in the white coat.

"It's just that last time… I hurt you. I… I didn't mean to."

Doctor Perkins reached for his right cheekbone and rubbed his fingers against it for a fleeting moment. A small grin pushed the flesh of his cheeks into them. He remembered their previous session.

"She's got a mean hook that one, hasn't she?" he joked, but across from him, the young woman remained still, stern-faced, whilst her eyes remained focused on him.

"That wasn't you," he reassured. "Ma'am doesn't play well with others, does she? But… I like to think we're past that now. Friends, almost."

He shrugged his shoulders.

"Maybe today's the day we shake on it."

A tender smile replaced the anxiety on Rhian's pale face. Her hands rose, free from their prison below, and rested well on the table. Doctor Perkins leaned his body until his chest was level with the tabletop, and his eyes peered up at Rhian's.

"Rhian shouldn't apologise unless Rhian did it," he whispered.

He never blamed her. Not once. He only ever tried to help, and as he sat back in his seat, he took note of how her shoulders began to relax. The anguish had washed away, and her breaths became lighter. Her eyes the whole time, remained fixed on the doctor.

One lengthened, steady breath.

*Okay*, she thought. I can do this.

The lights in the room began to dim at a crawled pace, like a torch in a narrow street that got further and further away. When all that remained was a gentle warm ambience, the doctor began to count backwards from three and held up a picture with his right hand, which shook a little.

It was a poster, black and white, and the only colour that bled from it was the centric title font.

THE SISTERS THREE

On the poster stood four women. Rugged and beaten, head to toe in military gear from the second world war. They stood in front of a mucky, slacked, and ripped tent. The kind of poses you'd expect; one arm on the hip while the other held a weapon, as they stared into an unseen distance. The woman that stood, hands on her hips behind the identical three, looked important. A leader.

Rhian's eyes froze as they fixated on the art, a look of recognition that became all the more distant. It provoked a keen interest from the doctor.

Her head leaned right in almost slow motion, and near rested on her dainty shoulder before it reversed its path and straightened out again. Her eyes snapped shut in an instant and for ticks on the clock, nothing. he sank into a slouch and let out a bothered huff.

"Well, you pick your stinkin' times don't ya'?" Her lashes lifted with the roll of her eyes. It wasn't Rhian anymore, not even close.

Doctor Perkins took a deep breath and leaned back into a more comfortable position. Chair pushed back, left ankle poised over the right knee. He recognised her.

"Hello Ma'am," he said. "Nice to see you again."

# 1

# IMPERFECT, PERFECT

Present Day.

Harley's hideout. It was their favourite restaurant. A building veiled with vines that playfully rattled in the late-afternoon wind. They crawled over its red bricks and under each dark frame that lined the windows. Modern, yet classic. It sat boastful between a line of smaller buildings, like the big brother it was.

Aaron and Rhian were tucked away in comfort at a fancy, cosy table in the back. Soft violin music played through tinny speakers that would crackle here and there, accompanied by the gentle chatter of the filled tables that surrounded them. The dimmed light complimented that which flickered from centrepiece candles throughout. It was as romantic as it was delightful.

Rhian sat with a smile that beamed almost ear to ear. Happy. Content. Feelings she'd gotten to know well over her eighteen months with Aaron. As she would on their 'date nights,' she wore her favoured red blouse, paired with black heels and trousers. The best-dressed woman in the room, as usual. She laughed as she looked at her partner.

"I'm not joking. Watch one, you'll see exactly what I mean."

"No, I agree… tasteful." Aaron wiped the remnants of food that hung in desperation from his thin-bearded chin and sprinkled down his white jumper. "But westerns are just… better than those period ones. Just how it is, sorry. Case closed."

Rhian nearly spat the delicious food from her mouth as she choked a laugh. She'd never heard him say something so… false. She reminded him of the last time he chose a movie. And that she fell asleep as a result.

Aaron took to a pause. "I have an idea."

"Ohhh, you have an *idea,* do you?"

"Has to be something out there that's got both right? Bit of you, a bit of me?" He folded his hand into the shape of a gun. Two aligned fingers pointed to his pursed lips, that sharply blew the invisible smoke from the barrel. He was a dork.

Rhian chuckled.

"Ten says I find something that fits the bill." Aaron reached his hand across the table and floated it above the plates.

Rhian shook his hand. "Ten it is."

She smiled and muttered under her breath how it would be the easiest ten she'd ever make.

Aaron noticed. "What was that?"

"Nothing," she shrugged.

She always did that; muttered just loud enough that he could hear it, yet quiet enough that nobody else could. All the while she'd pretend that she never said anything. A 'quirk.'

"A year and a half, almost, and you still think I can't hear that?" Aaron laughed. Rhian just shrugged. She was too busy with the next forkful of steak that graced her mouth and burst with flavour.

On the final swallow, she said, "Hey, question time... if you could change one thing from our past, what would it be?"

Aaron rested his jaw on his fist as he propped it on the table. He leaned into it.

"I don't know," he said. "I don't know if I'd change anything." He removed the prop from his chin and took another bite of his food. Through the hand that covered his mouth as he chewed, he re-trod history.

"Wouldn't change the first time I saw you…"

Rhian smiled at him before he could finish his sentence. "Because it took me forever to get them Weird Al tickets."

Her smile shifted to a playful frown.

"But also, because Bernice bought me that tray of nachos, so…"

He shrugged. It was a hard question, and he had a swarm of answers, none of which Rhian expected. Until…

"I wouldn't change a thing. We got where we are now, right? Change one thing, we might not be sat here today so I'll take it all as a win… The night I met you at that concert, the ups, and the downs since… all of it—"

Then it all changed.

Rhian shrank at her seat and bowed her head closer and closer to the table. The fork dropped from her hand and clanged against the edge of her silver-rimmed plate. As the other diners in the room perched up like meerkats, every unwanted set of eyes carried an unbearable weight. Her hands cupped tight across the front of her head, embarrassed and pained.

As if by memory, ignorant to the busybodies that snooped, Aaron gently placed down his cutlery and wiped his mouth, careful to make as little noise as he could as he stood from his chair. He moved to the other side of the table and bent down toward Rhian.

"Not good?"

She shook her head.

"You wanna pack up and go home, take a walk?"

In parallel, a nod.

Aaron looked around the room. From their part-eaten plates of food and barely touched glasses of wine to the onlookers and waiters who'd stopped what they were doing, just to observe. In mirrored fashion to times before, no second was wasted whilst the table and their belongings were packed up in near muted volume.

When he was done, Aaron gingerly slipped his hand under Rhian's arm and aided her up, then fixed her winter jacket over her. They left as soon as they could. A swarm of familiarity followed them like a shadow in the sun as twenty pairs of eyes glued to their exit. Unphased, Aaron's priority was the woman that clutched his hand, and *nothing or nobody else.*


They took a peaceful walk back to their lovely home, not thirty minutes down the road. It sat on what most considered one of the quietest streets of Devon. Its structure was highlighted by fanciful moonlight; the same luminosity that danced with golden gravel that dressed No.7's pathway. The streetlamps wore an orange glow as they lined the estate and added a dose of warmth to an otherwise cool night.

Rhian was mid-call with her cousin, Bernice as Aaron unlocked the door.

"I promise, Bernie" she insisted, as her head looked to the thin sprinkle of stars. "It was just another one of those headaches. The walk's helped me a lot… I feel better now. I know what you get like when I don't tell you these things, especially since I moved out."

Inside, as she swapped the phone from hand to hand, with somewhat of a struggle, Rhian managed to remove her jacket. She hung it at the bottom of the staircase where Aaron had kicked off his boots and left them in a lazy mess. A slight roll of her eyes; he always did that.

Having heard Bernice's worry a plethora of times, Rhian sighed. "I promise, if it gets too bad, I'll call Doctor Perkins. Scout's honour." She held her hand to the opposite side of her chest as she said it.

In the nicest way, she almost wished she'd never called.

As she entered the kitchen, she told her cousin she loved her too before she hung up and slid the phone across the clean counter and stood against it for a moment. Her hands wrapped on the edge with her fingers gripped on the underside of the black granite slab. The pressure increased, vice-like, and she began to wince.

Different was her character, as Rhian just stood stiff. Her big blue eyes glazed over, focused on the orange standby light of the kettle. As they began to close, her head tilted over to the right until *crack*! It thrashed quick - back into position and her knees buckled from beneath. It sank her body like a dead weight. Rhian's face became awash with fear and dread, eyes welled, on the verge of leaking over. Hot as liquid metal was the flesh on her face as it burned from beneath.

She cowered, terrified. A slow twist down, onto the hard, cold floor with her back married to the door of the cupboard. She tucked her knees into her chest as tight as she could and hugged them like a child would hug a plush toy, then eerily rocked from side to side.

"Go away." A slight break shook her voice. "Leave me alone." Then she faded deeper and deeper into the darkness that swallowed her.


It took several minutes, but eventually, Aaron strolled back downstairs. Robe on, he straightened out the boots he left stranded at the bottom, then called out for Rhian.

"Hey, did you see Dave's bakery was back open? Gotta stop by there and grab a pie one of these days don't you think?" He placed his hand on his stomach. "Missed that place."

He peered down the dark hall that divided the house. Nothing. So, he took a diversion to the kitchen instead. That's where he saw Rhian, vulnerable on the floor. The sway from left to right, the curled up tight-gripped huddle. The silence.

He'd seen her this way before, not that he saw any comfort in that. He looked for something in the room, and, as he clutched a piece of crumpled paper on the counter and snatched a pen from the top drawer below the kettle, he wrote something down. Something that took mere seconds, and he lay it down ahead of her feet on the black tile floor. He gently kissed her head before he disappeared from the room and down the hallway into another.

The only sounds in the entire building came from the obnoxious clock that would angrily slam the second hand into position, and the refrigerator as it hummed away in the background.

After sixteen long minutes, Rhian began to stir. She lifted her heavy head, slow until it thumped against the cupboard she'd sat against. A deep, strained sigh. Eyes opened, still red and watered, the tears she fought to hold back had left tracks down her cheeks with the specks of mascara they hauled with them.

A piece of paper lay on the floor in front of her. She picked it up, then cracked a smile as she read what was written.

WESTERNS ARE BETTER

She shot to her feet and headed straight for the living room, where Aaron was laid back at the head of the sofa, legs sprawled out and arms behind his head as he watched a game show on tv, his favourite pastime. He had it muted, with subtitles on, and mouthed the answer to the questions that popped up. Ones that he thought he knew, anyway. As smart as he was, he got one wrong. It triggered a snort.

"We still on this?" Rhian held up the piece of paper as she stood at the door.

Startled, Aaron threw his hand against his chest as his heart tried to escape and inclined at a speed that could have broken his back. He shifted his body to the edge of the seat to make room for her and padded a cushion with a few hefty slaps. Rhian put the note on the table centred in the room and ruffled into the gap he'd made. She kissed him on the cheek.

"I'll let you have it this time," she said as she rested her head on his warm chest. His heart was in a race, courtesy of her.

Aaron brushed the matted make-up away from Rhian's cheek.

"In my defence. Cowboys, guns, and duals," he imitated weighing scales with his hands, cowboys being the clear winner. "Or… overly pronounced Victorian English and *oh dear Willis where is my butler?*"

Rhian blurted out a laugh louder than she intended. She pulled it back into a snort as she tried to refrain from it with little success. "What was that supposed to be?"

"You and your period dramas."

"Willis where is my butler?" They both laughed.

Through her smile as it faded, Rhian asked who had 'shown up this time.'

"The quiet one… Whisper."

"How long?" Rhian tucked her exposed hair behind her ear.

"Fifteen minutes or something… just sat against the cupboard, rocking."

She hid it well, everywhere except her eyes. A clear reflection of worry spilt from them. Those other parts of her had never caused so much discomfort before. Ashamed, she caved to her self-hatred and asked, "How do you put up with me."

"Love." Aaron held Rhian just a little bit tighter. "I love you, you bloody idiot. Since day one." He kissed her forehead as he watched his show, with a little struggle while his head found the angle.

Rhian was convinced it wasn't that easy. Aaron knew it, just from her silence.

"It's difficult," he added. "It is, I won't lie, but I also won't push you away for it, like … it's… y- I know it's far more difficult for you.

Ember. Oh, Ember *hated* me, but whenever she comes out now it's different. Like we bonded a bit. They're part of you. Whatever rhyme or reason, *you*. I'm in your corner, I always will be. That goes for them too. I can handle 'em."

A heavy statement. Rhian took it with all the conviction she could. She'd never, in their eighteen months together, asked him that question. She was always too afraid that if he saw enough of her episodes, he'd eventually do what most others did, and leave her.

"You good now?" Aaron asked.

In denial, Rhian pressed her head further into Aaron's chest until the beats of his heart thumped their rhythm against her cheek.

"Yeah, I'm fine," she replied. "I'm okay."

It was the calm before the storm. Night soon slipped away, and early morning took its place. No sound outside but the breeze. It shook hands with the branches of trees that lined the street below. One particular branch clacked against the bedroom window as it fought back.

Rhian was in the midst of her roughest sleep to date, as she tossed and turned. It ruffled and kicked up the sheets into a loose mess. Beads of sweat ran down her face next to a sound-asleep Aaron. Rhian would sleep with her face pointed to the window, something about it relaxed her. Even still, her peace was disturbed. The odd panic or a jolt. It would last for moments and then fade into nothing. Then more, and the cycle continued as the hours melted away.

Eventually, her rough night woke the man next to her. He watched briefly, but then she began to thrash about in the bed, more violent than any time before.

Aaron inspected her bedside table from across the mattress. Placed in front of a picture of them both at a concert, stood a pill container. She'd taken her tablets; he could see two less in the brown bottle that once held four.

Something felt... off. As rough as Rhian would sleep sometimes, it was different... more erratic. Aaron began to fret. An attempt to calmly wake her was foiled by the fuel of her nightmares when Rhian sat up in a flash. She focused blindly on the mirrored door of the wardrobe opposite the bed. Through light smudges, she and the reflection stared at one another. Tranced and locked in a contest. Her head tilted to meet her shoulder before it sprung back.

Aaron helplessly watched, wide-eyed as the emotion drained from Rhian's face like water from a sink. She looked around, almost like she was lost, then her eyes met the man who stared right back.

In a thick British accent, she scoffed, "You've gotta be kiddin' me."

"Ember?"

"No, I'm your local bloody postman, why the hell ya starin' at me?"

It was hard to answer the question. Aaron wasn't even sure he had one to give.

Ember grew impatient.

"Right then, so I supp-"

The head of the woman tilted to her shoulder again – snapped back. With short, sharp breaths she began to panic and crawled back against the padded headboard. Like an attempt to protect herself from something, she buried her head deeper and deeper. She protected it with her arm as she frantically batted away at the unknown with the other.

In moments, she calmed. Her head lifted. Again, with the signature tilt and snap-back -- eyes locked once more on Aaron. She sat up tall.

"What?" she snapped in an unmistakable American accent.

"Which one are you?"

Nothing but a single tut came from her. Judgement at its finest. "Well, this is swell."

"I've never met you, right?" Aaron looked her up and down, his gears turned away, you could almost hear them grind, practically smell the oil they burned.

"You fancy me or something?" she barked.

In an instant, her head locked. One more tilt and her demeanour changed… it dropped her down until she was seated. She clasped her knees and rocked like a boat in waves. Just like she did in the kitchen.

"Whisper?" Aaron reached his hand out.

She whimpered. It got louder and louder almost like someone cranked a dial. It transformed into a loud, gleeful laugh filled with love and happiness, much like an excited child. It unsettled Aaron so much, he retreated further away to the edge of the bed. Then the laughter stopped on a dime.

One second. Two seconds of nothing until the room vibrated as she let out a harrowing scream that rocked Aaron so heavily, he scrambled off the end of the bed as if to take cover. It was horrific. It didn't stop until Rhian ran out of breath and steam. Then it faded like she'd been drained of her energy.

Everything relaxed, Aaron could feel Rhian come back as her face changed and her eyes opened again. The gravity in the room lessened.

She looked around and saw Aaron on his knees, posted up against the far corner of the bed… he looked like death, as pale as the duvet he clutched. She could hear the weight in his breath as it charged out of him with a lack of control.

Rhian padded the sweat from her forehead, then looked down at the covers. Messy, ruffled. She revisited Aaron's face… he didn't have to say anything.

"Who came out?" Tears started to well up in her eyes as her voice choked.

"I... You..." Aaron cleared the tight lump from his throat. "A lot."

"How many is a lot?" Tears jumped from her lashes to her cheekbones, then slid down to her fine jaw. "Aaron please."

Not knowing how to answer without hurting his darling's feelings, Aaron tried to dampen the tension with the only answer he had.

"More than I've ever met. Seconds... one after another. Then you screamed... I've never heard you scream like that before. I've never heard *anyone* scream like that before. I don't know what it was."

Rhian's blotted tears turned into streams that flowed down like a lake in the wind. Strong was the current. She couldn't stop them, not for lack of trying. She'd scared Aaron, she wasn't going to forget that. The fear he showed, the worry that chased her every outburst. That memory would follow her around on a short leash and pounce at a moment's notice. At this point, she couldn't even control the breaths she took. Each breath in was met with a judder, and each exhale a shiver.

Aaron climbed back onto the bed and approached her. Rhian's first response was to push him away but through his persistence, he found himself seated beside her.

"That bad dream you told me about, is it anything to do with that?" Aaron asked.

She'd explained that she had been having that same nightmare over and over for weeks, and it had gotten worse. A tall creature covered in fire, chased her through dark, endless corridors that led to nowhere until she'd wake. Though still, she shrugged it away as something unrelated.

She noticed the look in Aaron's eyes. She knew what it meant. What she had to do.

"I know." She paused. "I'll call Doctor Perkins in the morning." A statement that belittled her, even though it needed to be said, and done.

The man she thought she had scared away reached his arm around her waist and pulled her close. Her head rested on his shoulder and listened to every thud of his heart as it travelled through his ribcage. It settled Rhian like a lullaby would a child, and before they knew it, they were both sound asleep in the middle of the bed as the night slipped away once more.

The night of distress was but a memory and soon, birdsong began to override the silence. The light of the rising sun slowly lit up the bedroom with a bashful red glow, as it leaked through the crimson curtains that draped to just an inch above the floor. Everything in the room, from the wardrobe to the walls blushed as morning approached.

Three minutes to eight if the clock was to be believed, and Rhian began to wake – no… disturb.

"No," she whispered from within and begged something to leave her alone. Louder. The same plea repeated over and over. It got so loud that within minutes it woke Aaron.

As he sat hunched and rubbed the ball of his hands into his eye sockets, Rhian leapt from the bed with hers still closed. Her clenched fists pressed against her temples, and, as a heavy thinker would she began to pace up and down the gap beside the bed.

"Leave me alone," she begged. Sweat poured through her white nightgown in buckets.

It was clear to Aaron that she was in a fight with something, and the more fight it took, the deeper she went. His mind started to race as it tried to think of ways he could help, or if there were any.

Rhian's eyes opened, bloodshot and empty. From nowhere, she let out a scream that almost ripped her throat wide open. It lasted a lifetime until her breath expired, and she dropped to the floor in a lifeless heap.

Aaron shot off the bed in a hurry as if he were attached to a springboard. Unaware of exactly what the hell just happened, he begged for Rhian to wake up, only to go unanswered. The white of his eyes turned a salmon pink as the fire within his chest ramped up to eleven. His calls and his shakes did nothing despite the urgency within them.

His heart started to beat fast like a talking drum. His skin burned and his breaths accelerated into pants. He cupped his long, strong arms underneath Rhian's body and lifted her with a grunt chest height, then carted her out of the room. As light as she was, at that moment she weighed her most.

A careful swivel around the door frame, cautious to mind her head, then fourteen hollow thuds as Aaron descended the stairs one at a time with his love.

Straight to the living room, where just the night before they'd spent hours as a team who'd dominate late-night quiz shows, he extended his arms above the sofa and lay Rhian down, then double plumped a cushion beneath her head. He unfolded a throw-over blanket and covered her cold, bump-riddled legs.

Cold himself, Aaron was quick to gather his white jumper from the laundry basket in the kitchen. He threw it over his black bed-shirt then grabbed the jeans from beneath them. Clothed, he shot back to the living room where he hoped he had dreamt it all. Even warm, he froze.

The loud clock in the hall ticked away as Aaron stood in thought. What was he to do? He'd never come up against a situation quite like it in the time he was with Rhian, he didn't know how to handle it.

*Think, Aaron, think*. He considered himself useless. His panic blocked out any resolve until a single name came to him. Quick to gather Rhian's phone from their room, he scoured for her doctor's number in a frenzy with sharp swipes.

*Aha!* He found Felix Perkins and slapped his thumb against the screen to dial out. Just a few short seconds of dial-tone that at the time, felt longer than January, until a well-spoken woman answered.

Aaron was in no desire to have an extended conversation, despite her pleasantries. "Yeah, I need to speak to Doctor Perkins, please. It's urgent. My partner is hav--"

The hope washed away from his face as the receptionist informed him that Felix had passed away a few months prior. The dark clouds just wouldn't give up until the storm was in full play.

Aaron was curious if there was somebody else that he could speak with, but that, too, was met with a crushing disappointment. A short tap of the screen ended the call, along with his hope.

He placed the phone on the marble-effect coffee table, put his hands against his face and drove them back until it stressed his hair. His eyes jumped about like pinballs and shot from every surface from the floor to the ceiling.

Then, from the depths of his vision… a phonebook. It sat innocently on the shelf of the tv unit. Thank God they never threw that away.

With a glimmer of hope, like the smallest light in a pit of darkness, it was something to chase. Page by page, second by second, at a speed even Howard Berg would be proud of, Aaron found himself in the right section.

There was no time to be picky, his finger rested above an advert that caught his eye:

OSWALD JENKINS
UNORTHODOX PSYCHOTHERAPY
SPECIALIST IN PSYCHOLOGICAL DISORDERS
GET SEEN TODAY!

Perfect! He dialled the number with overwhelming anxiety and waited out another dial tone. His right heel tapped fast against the floor as he waited, and his nails shredded under the clamp of his teeth, but it didn't take long before somebody answered.

# 2

## THE ISLAND

Three gentle beats played on the dark wooden door. Aaron rushed to open it, and with a soft clunk and a weathered creak, it revealed a grey-haired man. Old and reserved, glasses that leant far down his bumpy nose, and a rather scruffy complexion like he hadn't bathed in weeks. The combined scent of tobacco and Old Spice invaded Aaron's nose. The guy knew nothing about personal hygiene.

"Oswald? Oswald Jenkins?" Aaron quizzed. He looked him up and down. This man was a doctor?

"Mr Haze, I presume?" Oswald looked at what he'd written on his hand, two different tones of ink like he'd added something later. "Must be the right place, where is the patient?"

Aaron urged the small fellow inside, and swiftly closed the door behind him. He snuck a crafty peek at the decrepit van that stained the view outside his home. To Aaron, that already made the man disreputable, but his choices were already thin.

In the living room, Aaron couldn't help but fixate on Rhian's unconscious state. It hung over him like a dense cloud. Oswald knelt beside her and remarked how staring wouldn't help, but it passed through Aaron's ears as if he'd never said a word. Nothing could make him feel any more helpless.

As he struggled to stand through the lack of co-operation from his unstable knees, Oswald positioned himself by Aaron and tapped his hand twice on his shoulder, the second of which, rested.

"It's alright," he said. "We'll have this figured out in a jiffy." He grabbed a yellow legal pad from his makeshift briefcase. The price sticker was still plastered across the front leaf, not one single page had been used. "Now, how long has Mrs Haze been in this state?"

Aaron's eyes pinged to the tv unit and lingered there for a while, "Harper." He cleared his throat then looked back. "*Miss* Harper."

"Apologies. Just an assumption." Oswald perched his glasses with a single finger.

"She's been like this for an hour and a half. Pretty much."

Oswald muttered to himself. Words indistinguishable, all a mumble. He placed two fingers across Rhian's dominant wrist and pushed them with the slightest pressure. The reflection of her face printed on his glasses whilst he took a moment to concentrate.

"Well, she's alive."

"Can you *help* her?" Aaron snapped. "Sorry. I'm just… I don't know where to start here, this has never happened."

"Yes, I can help. Many, *many* ways of helping. Tell me, Mr Haze, you mentioned a disorder on the phone. Personality? Bi-Polar? Can you elaborate please?"

Aaron took a seat in the small gap north of Rhian's head.

"D.I.D they call it. She has a few different ones… personalities. They come out randomly-"

"Not necessarily," Oswald interjected. "Not always random. Often, there's a trigger, like an emotion or a memory."

Aaron scratched the back of his head and scrunched his face.

"Not last night it didn't."

Oswald stood as straight as his back would let him, his hands glued to his hips. A look down to his empty notepad, another to Rhian.

"Go on," he urged.

"She's been having rough ones. Rough *sleep*. Nightmares. Sometimes she can't even get her head down to rest."

Aaron stood, shared a look at Rhian. A hesitation whilst he gathered his thoughts; he wondered if she'd appreciate him sharing her pain with a stranger. He shook his head and looked to the floor. He didn't exactly have a choice.

"Last night she lost it. One personality after another, five or six times. Maybe more, I don't know, I wasn't counting. Then she screamed… she sounded… possessed. It happened again this morning, but the scream was worse… and then…"

With the tilt of his head, Aaron's eyes diverted Oswald's to Rhian. "That happened."

The doctor's interest peaked tenfold. He was desperately high on the want for information. Oswald was curious how the personalities of Rhian, acted when they came out. "Violence or?"

"Depends," said Aaron. "The British one has an attitude, the American one speaks funny. I don't know, how does this help?"

"Every little bit helps along the way, Mr Haze. One last thing, these nightmares... of what exactly?"

Aaron had to think for a moment. "She told me it was a creature – a tall one, covered in fire, chasing her over and over again."

His description was loose, he only remembered what Rhian had told him, of which she was brief.

Oswald carried out a thorough inspection of Rhian. The rate of her breathing, her temperature. He peeled back the eyelid closest to him with the tip of his creased thumb and looked into her eye. To his surprise, there was motion. A dance within them, even. They bounced around like a ball in a box. Oswald shone a small torch that received no response as its bright glow met itself in the black of her iris.

"As I suspected," Oswald remarked. "There seems to be activity on the inside... plenty, yet nothing on the out."

Aaron felt sick to his stomach. A sensation that there was still no answer, nagged away at him. Perhaps he'd called the wrong person.

"I just wish I could help. She needs me."

Still busy with his examination, Oswald clicked off his torch and slipped it in the loose chest pocket of his oversized white shirt. It tucked into his jeans, probably to cover its size. His words hung on the tip of his tongue as it pressed against his teeth. A solid ten seconds passed until he figured he'd say them.

"Maybe you can," he tutted. "Come." And he left the room.

Aaron followed him with haste, outside the home to the less-than-great condition small van. Rust infected every door sill and hinge in his sight. The rear doors clunked, creaked, and moaned. They scraped as Oswald opened them. The noise was a demon to the ears, like nails on a chalkboard.

Aaron took a glance at the machine that sat centred on the bed of the van, padded in by battered cardboard boxes of paper and junk. The machine, a fair-sized bronze contraption, with vials strapped to either side and exposed gears and mechanics. It looked both antique, and futuristic at the same time, almost like something your grandparents would have lying around somewhere in their garage. The clear pipes that clung to it for dear life waged a territorial war with the trinkets that spilt from the boxes.

Oswald struggled as he shifted the mess. The device weighed almost as much as he did.

"Here," he grunted. "Help me with this."

Aaron waddled a reverse walk barefoot as he carried the machine through the house. He towed Oswald with him, his little legs were pulled along as they tried to match pace, unsuccessfully.

They placed it on the floor in the middle of the living room. Aaron's fingers slid from underneath with a sharp pull, and the machine thumped against the carpet as it closed the gap.

In his own little world, Oswald began to fidget as he set up the machine. He pinched a length of clear pipe, cut it into two with some tiny scissors, and fixed each length to a connection on either side. He cranked a lever, pushed a button. Then he ripped a pull-rope a good seven times before it fired up. It rattled, choked, and spluttered. One more crank, it started to shake and then a puff of steam rose until it became one with the ceiling. The constant wobbles and jitters were unsettling at best.

Aaron's eyebrows burrowed inward and clustered above his nose.

"What the hell is that supposed to be?"

Oswald smirked. "This, my boy, is a gift." He stood up with the help of the coffee table as it once more tried to support the weight under his feeble wrists. "A gift from my great grandfather. A little souvenir from 1939."

His amusement was weirdly out of place.

"Okay... but what *is* it."

Oswald held his head high. "Mind displacement bilateral bridge."

A cascade of confusion jacketed Aaron's face. Oswald took a more... *junior* approach.

"I can link yours and your partner's minds so you can *see* what's going on. Better?"

"Okay..." Aaron lifted his finger. "What?"

Oswald's frustration drew lines on his face. Through a pace and tone that insulted Aaron, he simplified the description further. It was a device that could place Aaron inside Rhian's mind where he could explore it... roam it. Much like a VR game, only he would be asleep in reality. Apparently, it was *completely safe.* Theoretically, a subconscious could take physical form, both from Aaron and Rhian, inside her mind.

"You want to save her, no? Be the hero? This is how you get there, Mr Haze."

"Oh, cool. So, I just strap in, do as you say and *boom*, Superman? Sorry if I'm just a little unconvinced."

Oswald did, however little, understand the man's disbelief. He'd never encountered anybody who'd reacted differently.

"You're not alone," he said. "Nobody ever believes in the impossible until they experience it."

Aaron rolled his eyes as he tucked Rhian's messed hair behind her ears. His worry held more volume alone than any words he spoke.

"Can't you just, I don't know... wake her up? Help her? I thought you were a therapist."

"Wake her up from what, exactly?" Oswald was keen to hear what Aaron thought he could do.

The words scrambled. A stutter shot from Aaron.

"Precisely," said Oswald. "My answer lies here." He pointed to his metal gizmo. "A definitive one, at least... right in your home."

He knew it, too. He'd spent the entire night wishing he could see what Rhian could, and the entire morning detesting his lack of answers.

"Fine, let's do it." No hesitation came from Aaron. He didn't know if it *was* safe, or even if any of it was real, he just remembered the words Oswald said; that he could save her. Any splinter of doubt left within him had been shunned with force.

The eyes of the doctor widened with joy. He rushed out to his van with a waddle and brought back with him two pint-glass sized vials of a less than healthy looking purple gas. His small hands had to cup them together in a desperate hold.

"Yeah, I'm not drinking that." Aaron turned his nose away.

Oswald chuckled. "Don't worry, that's not what it's for. However, if you're thirsty, I do hear there's water in the tap. Free, to an extent.'

Aaron's face lit up red as the blood rushed to his cheeks. He said nothing and watched the know-it-all do his thing.

Oswald removed the empty vials and snapped the new ones into place with a harsh click, then fed a clear pipe from one side, over into Rhian's nose.

Aaron was quick to question the logic as he cringed with its insertion. "You really have to jam that tube in her nose?"

"Do you think she can inhale this, consistently, for longer than say… an hour? On her own?" Oswald retorted.

"Fair enough." He looked at the clock. Nine-thirty.

Urged to, Aaron lay on the soft rug. Between the coffee table and the couch, as close as he could get to Rhian.

Oswald set up the second connection, and, as he dodged the cough it provoked, slid the clear pipe inches into Aaron's nose. He pointed to the amber light that flashed on his prized machine.

"You see that light, Mr Haze?"

Aaron sharply twitched a nod, careful of the pipe that poked away at his brain.

"When I press that, you'll start to feel a little… strange as the chemical enters your system. Don't fret, it's normal. Close your eyes and count to fifteen, let the machine work its magic. You'll find her, she's in there somewhere. You'll bring her home… you have my word."

Another nod from the nervous man.

Oswald reached for the button and flicked it down with his index finger. It locked into place and turned from an orange blink to a steady bright red. The violet gas started to thin and travelled down the clear pipes and into the couple's airways.

Aaron did feel strange. It felt like dizziness… stronger than any he'd ever experienced, like a heavy dose of vertigo. It almost made him throw up.

"Wait." He struggled to get the words out. "How do I leave?" Aaron's eyes drifted shut and his chest flattened as his body relaxed.

"How do I leave?" Oswald repeated, to an unconscious Aaron. He looked to the machine as it hissed and puffed away then followed the purple mist through the pipes, back to the couple.

"The popular question."

Everything was distorted in silence. Aaron pushed out a long sigh as he twitched his head.

"Doc, I don't think this is working."

Irked, he opened his eyes, then immediately narrowed them under the bright light that invaded his view. It took a moment to adjust, but eventually, it settled. He quickly patted his body down, and to his delight, he was perfectly fine.

As he pushed his hands against the cold hard floor, he took a sharp breath in and scanned around.

Dirty, flaked, red-painted concrete floors, unkept and beaten lay beneath his feet. Scuffed white walls just as much an ogre to the eyes, littered with cobwebs and wounds. They housed a row of windows, and as he pushed forward, his footsteps birthed an infinite echo. He noticed the decayed iron bars that were vertically bolted over the windows, much like those in a prison cell. It was dark and lonesome; it screamed abandoned. Nothing there besides a hefty steel door at the furthest end as he turned left around the only corner he was given.

As goosebumps turned Aaron's arms to sandpaper, he opened the door. It was heavier than he imagined and took some shoulder strength to swing it wide. It bounced off the metal rails that lined the three steps down and slammed shut behind him with a bass-riddled boom.

Murky and miserable, but at the same time beautiful and otherworldly, the dock that sat thirty feet ahead of Aaron was swallowed by fog as the white sky had fallen lazy upon it. It looked mystical, like the everglades in the dawn of winter. Mesmerized, Aaron took note of the towering structure in the distance that pierced through it. Some kind of building, that's all he could make out, as the view he was dealt with, hid the details.

His skeleton began to rattle beneath his skin as the raw breeze pushed against him, and every breath left a thick vapour in its wake. Each one, a ghost of a breath that once was.

Aaron shouted into the hazy abyss and anticipated… rather, hoped for a response. A sign that anyone else was there. But all that called back was the return of his own hello. Disoriented, he shivered more and more, so Aaron chased back the footsteps he left in the shin-height brittle grass and headed back inside the building where he'd be warmer.

*That's strange*, Aaron thought as he walked inside, the building had become littered with a line of doors opposite the windows, that took attention from the unsightly walls. Each door was different in colour as Aaron walked past them and tried to make sense of it all. Six doors, he counted.

By reflex, Aaron tried the knob of the blue door. Blue was his favourite colour, so it was worth a shot, but it was locked. Nothing but clicks and rattles as the door stood ignorant before him.

*Alright,* he thought, then tried a few more.

It took him longer than he'd ever like to admit before he realised only one single door was unlocked: the orange one.

He gathered his composure and turned the knob with care. With no inclination of what to expect, he took each step slow as he walked through.

If only he'd known whose door he'd just opened, it might have saved him the panic.

# 3

## EMBER

A cup of lukewarm tap water. That's what the dense air tasted like as it punched its way into Aaron's lungs. It was a strange feeling, almost like he forgot how to breathe.

He felt the tall, damp grass engulf itself around his shins, and each foot he took forward tore it from its roots. The strength each step took was tiresome, more and more so.

Aaron looked down as the forces released and he started to slide forward, almost like he'd stepped on some ice. His once-clean boots were lathered in liquid mud which collected at his toes in an ugly pile that only grew with every slide.

"Gross." He took a moment to kick the soles repeatedly against the broad trunk of a nearby tree. It chipped away at the bark with every impact. Seven thuds and a splattered mess, then Aaron's ears perked up.

Through the creaks and snaps as branches of lanky woodland trees tussled with the unkempt shrubbery that swallowed them, and past the musical notes of birdsong, Aaron could recognize the sound of gushing water anywhere. He'd never moved so fast yet so careful. To hell with the vines that snagged his shoulders as he tackled through them.

There it was, right in front of his eyes. A wide stream that fell fifty feet. A relaxing flow of infinite… lava.

As any normal person would, Aaron aimed a stare at the unknown, nursed with squinted eyes.

"Really?" A sharp exhale from deep within his chest, matched the tone of the thrashing ahead of him. "Lava? Sure, why not?" He muttered.

As the view took him hostage, he gazed upon the beauty of it for a while as his mind attempted to assemble the madness in wonderful ways, unaware of what crept up behind.

Cold was the thick barrel that rested against the base of his neck. An unsettling yet somehow nice sensation given the situation.

"So… can I turn around yet?" He held his hands nonchalantly above his head, beads of sweat lined up above his brows.

The barrel pushed firm, enough to jerk Aaron forward an inch or two. Its wielder wasn't there to mess around.

"Who the bloody 'ell are ya? How'd ya get in 'ere then?"

Aaron's ears danced. He recognized that hefty British cadence anywhere. His hands dropped aloof and slapped against his thighs.

"Ember?"

In his slow turn, he made note of the woman's barely together bunker boots and unzipped, casually sat leather jacket. It stole a peek at the dirtied white shirt that sat underneath. Rhian, but not Rhian. The first alter he ever met.

He arched back his head as he faced her and placed his index finger on the barrel of the flamethrower she pointed at him, then pulled it down from his face, slow, with a soft chuckle.

"Cold, ironically," he joked.

"Aaron?!" she snapped with a locked jaw and pressed teeth. Her shoulders shot to and from her neck so sharp they forced the bottom of her short-cut hair into a bounce.

Ember and Aaron had interacted many a time in the real world, but she never once imagined him in hers.

"How then," she said. "Come on." She flexed the strap on the flamethrower and slung it over her shoulder like it weighed nothing.

"You wouldn't believe me if I told you." Aaron straightened the dirtied jumper he'd started to sweat through.

Ember took her eyes off Aaron and locked them to the river of lava he had just spent ten minutes staring at.

"Right… good point," he withdrew. "Can we go somewhere else? I'm sweating buckets here."

She did have somewhere: a hut just a short walk from where they were, a small one, but one that mattered. A place she called home. She led him there, after some mild hesitation, through muddy paths that split through groups of marigold flowers and daisies. Ember couldn't help but reach her hand out to the flowers as she passed them. She was fond of this place.

She was never the quiet kind, so she made sure to repeatedly announce her surprise that Aaron had suddenly shown up out of the blue. The man never got a chance to respond.

Before he knew it, Aaron found himself surrounded by a ring of huts that sat atop dusty, murky gravel. It was a place perfectly suited for a jungle dweller.

Each hut was shredded and collapsed from the roof down, and most of them were fully coated in black charcoal scars. All torn and dishevelled, minus one; the one Ember called home.

It still had taken somewhat of a beating, but it was clear why she chose it. It was the biggest, but also the homeliest. Ember did what she did best and worked with what she had.

Aaron took in the rotted, barely-together mass of straw and wood as he stepped inside. The smell of dampness confronted him, and the floor cracked and bowed beneath his feet. There wasn't much to the inside. It was bare-bones, but it worked.

*She lives here?* he thought. He wondered how she ever got by, then quickly remembered the stubborn, tough woman he had followed. Ember was no joke.

He picked a seat from the line of crates that sat left of him and lined the wall, and asked, "Have anything to drink?"

The tin can scratched against Aaron's lip as he drank from it. It was hardly a mug and had *clearly* been opened by a ravaging wolverine… but it served its purpose and held whatever it was he drank. It looked like water, tasted like water, but it sure didn't smell like water.

"Thank you," he said. The drink sputtered through his lips as he sipped it.

Ember parked a seat at the wooden picnic table central to the hut. It acted like a dining table for her, though she'd choose to sit on the top, rather than the seat. "Storytime, Haze. Waiting."

He sighed. "Yeah, about that. I'm not even certain about that."

Ember tilted her head. Aaron noticed, he reached a hand in front of him, palm out.

"Give me a second. What I mean is I don't know how I got here exactly. Well, I know how, I just don't know…*how.*

"There was this doctor, science guy right. Jenkins… seemed like a nice guy… pretty old. He had this machine-"

"Hold on a minute there, Hamilton, you're lapping me here. Doctor?" Ember rotated her finger anticlockwise.

"Yeah, Jenkins. I called him." Aaron's eyes dropped to his feet. "That Felix doctor that was good with Rhian… he's not… well he's not *about* anymore."

"About?" Ember asked.

All it took was the one look from Aaron and she knew. At this point, she could read his face pretty well.

"Shit," she exhaled. "Rhian?" She started to scratch the tip of her short nails through the grain of the table as she took a sip of her drink.

"I haven't found her yet, I just got here."

The water in Ember's mouth shot out like runners to a starting pistol with so much force she almost choked.

"Haven't found- the fuck you mean you *haven't found her yet*?" With the cuff of her jacket, she wiped the droplets of spilt liquid that hung from her chin for dear life.

"As I said, I haven't been here long. Haven't really had time, Ember. I wired up to the machine, woke up here, walked half a mile then you pushed the barrel of a flamethrower into the base of my skull."

"Sorry about that," she shrugged. She wasn't sorry, she'd have found it funny. "The machine brought you here?"

"Yeah."

"A machine you just, what…" she twisted her wrist until her free palm faced the ceiling. "I'm guessin' you didn't really think it through."

Aaron didn't have to say anything. The hesitation from him alone, told Ember what she already knew.

"That doctor, he told you it'd save her. Nailed it, ain't I?"

"Yeah, bu—"

"For Christ's sake, Haze! You don't even know what you got yourself in for! Do you even know what this place is?"

Aaron looked around the hut. He remembered the doors and the lava, that was about it. He looked at Ember.

"Not exactly… but, Oswald said something about being able to… see inside Rhian's head. That's this, right? I'm inside her head…" His finger aimed at her. "You're here."

Ember bit her tongue, hard. Enough that the pain of it could swipe her words away but that was wishful thinking.

"Listen…" she rolled her tongue left to right over her bottom lip. "I know you're the kinda idiot to chase a hero title, but did you think about anythin' before you came here?"

"Well, yea—"

"No," Ember snapped. "You heard what ya needed to and you said, 'let's do it,' because that's what you do."

Aaron froze. He'd forgotten that Ember knew him as well as he knew her. He sat still on the crate he'd chosen as his seat and drew blanks instead of answers.

Ember nodded with a cocky smile. She knew she had him dead to rights. "This… machine, it can take you back, right? Look, I like ya, you're a good one but this place, it ain't for ya, Haze. You want answers?"

She pointed to the battered straw roof above her as she stood. "Then you go back up there, you find another shrink and you help her. There's nothin' in here that'll help ya, mate."

Aaron squoze the aluminium tin in his hand until it bent slightly, still half-full of water, and threw it sharp ahead of Ember as she walked away. It clanged against the wooden slats that made up the wall and sat in a crumpled mass.

She stopped in her tracks. Only her head and neck turned back to face him, it creeped Aaron out. It reminded him of a doll from those horror movies Rhian liked to watch.

"I'm exactly where I need to be." He stood firm in his place and gestured to the very same battered roof. "Up there, out there? All there is... is my body lumped on the floor, strapped to some 'doctor's' steampunk toaster, less than two feet from Rhian's body in the same damned place I left her after she passed out!"

He turned his head to the side and swallowed the lump that was trapped hostage in his throat.

"She never woke up. I'm sorry, Ember. I never meant to come in here and get in the way. I'm just trying to save the woman I love. I don't care what it takes. The way she went out this morning, something isn't right."

Ember took a step back as her nostrils flared and her eyes began to water. Of all the things Aaron could have said, she didn't see that one coming. Who could have?

Aaron's heavy breath lasted a lifetime as his chest rendered him heavy.

He whined, "Maybe you're right, maybe I should be back out there. I'm just messing it up, that's what I do. Every time I think I'm helping, maybe I'm just making it worse."

It took all his strength to pick his burdensome head up and cross eyes with Ember.

"It was my panic that led me here. It led me to a stranger wiring me up to some kind of… machine. Led me to… I don't even know, I'm still trying to process it all, you know?"

Ember found a gap in Aaron's breakdown and seized an opportunity.

"When she blacked out… Rhian, did she say anythin' or what?"

"Not really, she was trying to get away from something I guess, screaming. You came out."

"You what?"

"You don't remember?"

Ember frowned. She had no idea what Aaron was talking about, which made everything awkward. She never left; she'd have known if she did.

"I thought you did. Maybe I mistook you for one of the others."

She doubted that very much. She and Aaron knew each other well at that point, there wasn't a single chance that he *mistook* her identity. She brushed it off; it was clear he wasn't in a good place.

"So, there's nobody up top right now? Like, at all?"

"No one."

She prayed she heard him wrong and shared a look across the room for longer than she intended, in hope that it was a sick joke. But everything came back to the same answer; nobody was in control of Rhian, not even Rhian herself.

"Okay," she said. "Tell me everything, and don't you leave a damn thing out."

Not that he already wanted to relive the night's events for the third time, Aaron pushed away his pride and released a flow of information that would leave Ember, for the first time in her existence, lost for words.

She rummaged around inside her head as she tried to make sense of it all, but much like the man who sat across from her, she had nothing.

Aaron saw something familiar in the way Ember acted.

"That feeling," he said. "That's exactly what I feel. No answers or anything. Useless. I should just walk right back through that door as you said. I can't help her in the one moment she needs me. Great, aren't I?"

Ember wanted to say something, but she couldn't. She took a breath and nodded her head in pattern while she sucked against her teeth. She looked to the wall behind her: a square-cut hole in the side of the hut, with a piece of wire mesh, tacked to it with a handful of rusty nails. She called it a window.

"Okay." She turned her head to a door just a few feet from the window. "Follow me."

They'd walked nearly fifteen minutes north of the hut. Well, to Aaron it seemed more like a hike. Up steep slopes carved into the sides of almost vertical hills, and across wooden plank bridges suspended by a questionable rope above deep drops into streams of running lava. The journey tested him, but if anything, it was proof that his fitness wasn't nearly at the level he thought it was.

Ember's silence for the entire journey had Aaron locked behind a wall of nerves but regardless, he followed her until they finally stopped at a monster of a hill-climb. Easily a twelve-foot almost vertical mound of grass and rock.

In awe, Aaron watched as Ember scaled the bank with zero trouble and minimal effort. She threw him down a withered climbing rope that was anchored at the top with a sizeable metal spike. It has been there forever; he could tell by the rust that coated it.

He pulled himself up, best he could, and almost tore his shoulder along the way. At the top, he needed a few minutes to gather himself. His breath had absconded from him, and his arms and hands were sore with blisters.

Ember rolled her eyes. She'd never seen anything so pitiful, and as the lacklustre climber rose to his feet atop the mound and peered over the opposite side, his jaw dropped while his body froze.

Eighty, maybe one hundred feet. That's how massive the drop was from the top to the bottom of a mesmerizing waterfall of the same bright lava that stumped him as he entered the world. It crashed and fought with itself steep at the bottom within its own pool and created walls of orange that rippled out to the edges. Breath-taking for someone like Aaron, he sunk straight back down. The strength stolen from his legs forced him to sit.

"This is what you brought me here for?" He asked with a dry mouth. "It's amazing."

Ember sat beside him, cosy. "It is to you," she said. "Me, I come 'ere and remember."

"Remember?" Aaron watched as, for the first time, he saw an ounce of vulnerability on the British woman's face.

"I remember it all. We all do... what happens up there. Only with muggins 'ere, the memories are never bad. At least not since the first time I found this place."

Aaron's soft eyes never left her. Pinned down to a moment of sharing and reflection, he was all ears.

"Went from seein' her walk into that fire over and over again, thinkin' I'd never escape it... to rememberin' every damn time your stupid ass just wouldn't give over."

Aaron glanced to and from the glowing falls as they hissed and collided in the backdrop.

"Her?" he asked. "In the fire... Rhian?"

Ember shook her head gently and clenched her jaw so tight it ground her teeth. She didn't want to say too much. She didn't want to be reminded of it all again. A name was all she said.

"Lynn."

"Who's Lynn, Ember?"

But Ember repressed so much more than Aaron could ever contemplate. Cryptic in her response, she simply told him it was somebody she used to know.

"That's not the point," she continued. She guided Aaron's sight to a gigantic tree that sat opposite the steaming pool below. A large, thick branch hung from the side, broken.

"I used to sit there, on that branch, and hope that one day it'd break, and take me with it. You know, put me out of my misery. Take away everythin' that was messin' with me. Instead, it broke when I left. It was like it knew."

"You wanted to die?"

Ember bowed her head above her bent up knees and spoke to the floor.

"Once… Mate, we all did."

"What changed your mind?"

She picked her head up and looked directly at him. "You did."

Aaron didn't understand. He wondered how he, of all people, could have changed anyone's mind about something so… dark.

Ember dropped what was left of her guard. She knew Aaron was beating himself up, just as well as she knew the kind of man he was.

"Sixteen months ago, I sat 'ere, in this very spot. Right after I came back from out there. You know what happened?"

Aaron looked blank. Ember responded with a smirk.

"You and Rhian had been knockin' about for a couple of months, until one night, the California Wildfires were all over the news. I know, 'cos it's the reason I was chosen to go up there… protect her from it. First time I met ya'."

"First one that spoke back," Aaron joked.

"Weren't fond of ya. *But…* even though I was a dick to ya, you saw exactly how that shit on the tv affected me. You asked for my name, then fiddled about with ya' phone, turned off the TV and blasted that song… Ember to Inferno, on repeat, until I forgot about everythin'. Ended up back in 'ere."

Aaron let a small laugh slip from his nose as he smiled. "Yeah, I remember that."

He remembered the pain he saw in her eyes as the flames on the TV reflected from them. He recalled being labelled an ass as he turned it off.

"At first I thought you was takin' the piss," she said. "Then I came here, sat down, and realised… you'd helped me forget somethin' that would've made me wish that branch was still there."

Aaron looked at the branch as she did. His mind started to cycle back in time… it rewound, and he remembered something Ember said.

"Protect her."

"What?"

"You said you were chosen to protect her…Rhian, from what?"

Ember pursed her lips. "Remembering."

Aaron geared up to say something else, but with a signal from her finger, Ember stopped him. She wasn't done just yet.

"Another time I went up top, the first thing I saw was a bakery, flames rippin' through it, and we were standin' right outside it, watching. You looked at me… realised it was me, not her… saw how badly I wanted to help the people that were screamin' and what did you do?"

"The bakery, right? Dave's? We went inside."

Ember nodded with a pleased smile. "Yeah. You put your jacket over my head, and we went in. Helped those people out of the back, and your lungs paid the price."

"I did," Aaron said. "I remember you thanking me."

"Ya helped me." She looked deep into Aaron's eyes. She was thankful even to that day.

"That's my point, Haze. That's why I brought you 'ere. All you do is help... can't stop yaself. You sat in my home and told me how ya think you're messin' it all up. Bullshit.

"You, and you alone, changed how this stubborn arsehole looks at the world when she's out there.

"Don't matter if it takes a while, don't matter if you put yourself in harm's way, just... did it. Got on with it. I know exactly why Rhian loves ya."

"Yeah?"

"You're constant. A rough one comes out and thumps you in the throat, I'll bet twenty you just roll with it."

"Twenty?" Aaron raised his eyebrows. "Big bets. Never went above ten with Rhian."

With a warm smile, Ember placed her hand around the back of Aaron's head.

"You're right there when she goes through the rough ones, Haze. Every time. You're the only damn person who ever loved her and proved it. No ulterior motives, no doubts."

She slapped her free hand against his chest.

"Just a big heart, yeah? You're good. Good for her, and good as you. You wanna help her, then go out there and help her... may as well now you're here. And when you find her, you tell 'er I'm the reason you grew some balls eh?"

The pair stood and hugged at the top of the embankment. A warm embrace of friendship. More so with the vista of lava and steam ahead of them.

"I might not like the fact you're in 'ere," she said. "But if the answers are here too... wouldn't put it past ya to find 'em."

Ember only ever respected Aaron, and, on that day, she lay it all on the line and told it how it was. It didn't matter that she didn't agree with his methods, not as long as she knew his intentions. That, she did. Aaron didn't have a bad bone in his body.

They stood up ready to return, and Aaron smiled.

You know, Dave's Bakery is open again."

"Really?!" Ember shouted. It reverbed through the area that surrounded them. "He still doin' them steak bakes?"

"You bet."

"See," said Ember, in approval. "Can't let a little fire hold ya back."

They retraced their steps back to the hut, in a journey that Aaron found much easier in reverse. Past the ring of huts and back through the pathways and mud, the pair stood next to the door that started it all and shared one final farewell.

Ember held her muddy hand out to Aaron. "All things considered... glad ya came here, Haze."

He shook it with a grip so firm it impressed her. "Me too."

He turned to twist the scratched silver knob of the door and cracked it open no further than a couple of inches.

"Oh, the door with the bow..."

Aaron stopped opening the door and turned to face Ember.

"Do yourself a favour and maybe don't go in that one yeah? 'less you like havin' a knife stuck in ya chest."

"That bad? Really"

"Let's just say there's one or two of us you're gonna wanna just skip over. There's such a thing as too much. Consider it a friendly warnin'."

Aaron saw the seriousness that dressed her. "Gotcha," he said. "Door with the bow, no-go."

Ember nodded. "See ya around, Haze."

"Yeah, see you around, Ember"

With an exchange of smiles, Aaron opened the door and disappeared into a harsh white void. As the door shut behind him, it slowly faded into nothing as Ember watched by, and hoped that he would be safe... but she also knew deep down that he would do the right thing.

Aaron narrowed his eyes as the white mess around him began to cease and his surroundings became visible once more. Stood in the stretch of building, littered with doors, he immediately noticed the orange one had vanished. His access to Ember's world was gone, and he wondered what was next.

He looked up and down the row of doors. Light blue, white, black... No bow on any of them, maybe Ember was mistaken. One by one he tested the handles. It didn't take him long to find the next available door.

He turned the knob of the pale-blue one. It clunked as the latch disconnected, and a ray of sunlight burst into his view from the very first inch it cracked open. Aaron guarded his eyes with his arm and pushed forward through the entry.

*Here we go again,* he thought, as the door closed behind him. Here we go again, indeed.

# 4

## DOLLY

The white arch stood eight feet perpendicular as it lined the perfect-cut, flawless green grass with grace. So perfect it almost looked fake. No single blade of grass was longer than the other.

Butterflies of all colours danced around in the bright blue sky that looked between the crossed beams of the arch, which had at most, a handful of light clouds sprinkled through it.

For almost five full minutes, the path birthed of green led Aaron deeper and deeper into a glorious new world, until eventually, it opened up into a full field of the same, pure grass. Complimented with dandelions and a vast colour palette of poppies, it carried the ground to a vista of trees as it merged into a forest that looked like something only a fairy-tale would offer.

Above the forest, in the far distance, a light-brick castle, complete with pointed, blue columns, proudly peeked above it all. The new world was something else entirely. From the first inch, it felt mythical.

Aaron took a moment to think. Whose world had he stepped into? Through how innocent and dainty it all felt, his mind was left blank.

As he progressed down countless acres of perfect field, careful to mind his feet on the pretty floral decorations it wore, he slowly advanced to the entrance of the magical forest.

Past tall, bright trees in which birds sat to nest their chicks and sang them a blissful harmony. Through small streams that separated the mud with their gentle currents over smooth, rounded rock beds. Like something from a child's book, everything floated within the realm of ethereal.

Then, the cottage appeared.

It was cute and modest. Aaron maintained a distance as he scouted around for any movement, or a sign that anyone was there, but there was nothing, until a rustle from the bushes to his left, startled him.

Aaron's edge softened, and his head remained turned down as it followed a squirrel to the tip of his feet, where it rested.

The squirrel's eyes closed part-way as Aaron stroked it front-to-back with the face of his thumb.

"Hey there, little fella," he said, hushed. "Where did you come from?"

Ignorant to his question, the squirrel bolted off in the opposite direction and disappeared far into the foliage. For something so small it packed a lot of speed.

Aaron shrugged. He decided to check out the cottage some more. The closer he got, the more surreal it seemed to feel.

Beautiful and well-kept. White-painted stone walls that reflected the midday sun onto the trimmed flowerbeds that lay lined the underneath windows, neat and full of life. A golden gravel path sprawled into empty stables on the left and spilt over to meet the grass-floored garden orchard like the most elegant of welcome mats.

As Aaron crept left and stood by at the stable, he noticed a female figure deep in the orchard. It was obvious by the trim that flared of the pastel-blue summer dress she wore. She held a basket in her hand as she stretched tall and picked the plump red apples off the beautiful trees.

"Excuse me!" he shouted.

The young woman turned to face him and walked to him with a clutch of her basket. Soon, it was plain to Aaron that this was *exactly* who he was supposed to meet.

Rhian's face, bordered in a wavy brown flow of hair that rested on her shoulders as it leaked from beneath her straw summer hat. Daisies were pinned in a row around the brim of it. She had a spring in her step as she crossed the threshold of grass and crunched her feet against the warm gravel.

She gasped, "Hello!"

Excitement rushed her like a sickness, and she wasted no time as she placed the basket on the floor. A couple of bright red, plump apples spilt out, but she didn't care. She ran to Aaron and hugged him tight - so tight and bent her left leg out behind her until her toes pointed back to the orchard. For someone who lived in such a sunny world, she sure was pale-skinned.

"Oh, my first visitor," she cheered as she released the uncomfortable man. "What's your name?"

"I'm Aaron. Pretty sure we've never met, right?" He pointed to the clouds. "Up there?"

The Rhian doppelganger missed his question in her glee.

"Aaron, I like that. I like that name! Say, you want an apple, friend?" She clapped her hands the fastest she could. "They're the best in the world!"

With no want to upset her, Aaron accepted the offer as she passed over one of the reddest apples that he'd ever laid eyes on. With a little hesitation, he took a wide bite from the side. To his joy, she was right.

"Hmph, one of the best apples I've ever had," he said as he licked his lips. The juice ran down his chin. He was quick to wipe it with his sleeve, though a bit annoyed when he saw the dirt that had collected on it from his trip into Ember's world. He shook at it until all the loose bits dismounted.

"I'm sorry, which one are you?"

"My name's Dolly." She slung out the frill of her dress with a pull of her hands as she leaned forward. Only the finest courtesy for her visitor.

"You here to help me find my friend?" she asked, excited.

The question stumped Aaron. He scratched his head and fumbled for an answer.

"Maybe," he said. "Is your friend Rhia-"

Dolly cut him off with a delighted laugh. She danced around in the sunlight and flicked her clean, white heels up. It turned up and scattered the stones beneath them.

Aaron couldn't help but wonder why Dolly was so happy and full of life. Why would a part of Rhian so happy, have been separated from her? Everyone he'd ever met was burdened to deal with something that dragged them down.

Dolly centred her concentration with a cough, aware she'd veered off into her own little world again.

"Sorry, friend!" she shouted. "Where were - oh! You're gonna help me, right?" A grin so sharp it revealed her teeth. It reminded Aaron of a child.

*Wait a minute,* he thought. *Maybe that's it!*

In concert with Dolly's innocent demeanour, Aaron heightened the register of his voice and added a certain... elation to the way he spoke.

"Hey," he said. "Where's your friend then?"

"Don't know," she giggled. "That's what *lost* means."

Point taken. Aaron probably should have thought about that a little bit more.

"Let me rephrase. Pick a direction... and we'll go that way. An adventure!"

Adventure? The word itself was enough to spark Dolly into her brightest light yet. She covered her mouth with married hands and amidst her inward gasp, let out a small squeak.

"Adventure?! For reals? Or are you pulling my little leg?"

"Wanna go?"

Of course, she did, and time was now of the essence. Never mind the apple-picking and never mind any further questions. She pointed deeper into the forest.

"Ten-Hut!" she yelled, as she imitated a soldier's marching orders with a forced rasp, then strolled off past the front of the cottage and into the trees.

It took a light jog for Aaron to catch up with her.

Through endless rainbow-coloured poppy fields and wildlife-ridden treelines where Aaron would stop to pet *all* the squirrels and critters, he and Dolly came to a clearing. It only took two hours, or at least, that's what it felt like. Aaron was once again reminded that he needed to work on his physical health. The spring-stepped woman he followed had a pace that threw his to the wind. She didn't say much, she was too distracted by her eagerness.

They cleared the trees and crossed a plain acre of grass before they were confronted with a thick blanket of snow. The sky above them had a clear perfect line between the blue sky and the white, cloudy mass like somebody had drawn it there with a ruler.

With careful steps that crunched beneath them, they decided to keep moving forward. It took a toll on Dolly's fragile shoe heels. One snapped, and it dragged her foot down further into the sheet of white sky crystals.

"Oh no!" she squeaked.

"What's the problem?"

"Oh… my heel broke." Her bottom lip pushed out, then she laughed. She took off her shoes and placed the broken heel inside one.

"Silly shoes."

Aaron looked down at her feet. No socks, barefoot, inches deep into even deeper snow. The skin that wrapped them turned blue with every bite of the hungered frost.

He bent down, slipped off his muddied boots and placed them in front of her.

"Put them on."

"Oh you," Dolly blushed. "Don't be so silly."

"Please." At least he had socks on.

Dolly took note of the look Aaron shared. He *really* wanted her to wear his boots. To please her new friend, she put them on, and she was glad. They were comfortable.

"They're a bit…big."

Aaron masked his scoff with a chilled breath. "Give it time, you'll grow into them." He took a solid look at the happy woman and couldn't help but inquire.

"Hey," he continued. "So, what's with… well, this?" He turned his palms up and looked around.

"What?" Dolly giggled.

"The…" Aaron pushed out air from puffed cheeks. He tried to figure out how to word it. "The bright colours and the… joy. Now we're in snow all of a sudden."

Dolly laughed again. "It's always been like this. It's why I *love* it." She adjusted her feet in the boat sized boots. "Do you like it?"

"Of course. It's… different. In a good way. I Just expected more... I don't know… drama."

"Why?" She never took a blink whilst she waited for his answer.

"Just, seems to come with the territory. I mean… pretty sure that – what am I saying?" He rubbed his finger and thumb down the bridge of his nose. "I just figured that maybe it was bad things that made you guys."

Dolly diverted her attention to a non-existent distraction far to her right.

"Hey," said Aaron. He snapped his fingers a foot from her face. "Anyone in there?"

"So! What's things like out there? For you?" she asked. She totally didn't change the subject.

Aaron played along. "At the moment, a little rough." He took a long bite from the inside of his cheek. "I'm working on it."

With his encouragement and a note of how long they'd walked for, they continued their journey.

Their trek lasted forever as Dolly's feet slid back and forth inside the boots that were five sizes too big, they started to rub at the sides of her feet. Her being as she was, she never said a word about it.

In a similar fashion to the journey, the vista of snow seemed to last an awfully long time, not that it mattered to Aaron, his feet became numb to it. Quite literally, so he also said nothing.

Just as his impatience started to creep, he noticed something in the distance. Something that sat just yards ahead of the pointed castle they'd neared.

"What's that?" he asked Dolly. The tune she was whistling came to a delayed stop.

She looked. She noticed the snow thin out to a seemingly solid, smooth surface. "Ha, that's called ice, genius!"

Just as Aaron thought, it was never going to be over. The sub-zero ground they trod could have at his feet for all he cared. Not that he needed them or anything.

At last, the slew of ice neared its end. Aaron's brick feet barely felt the soft, muddy grass that began to emerge, blade by blade. It was disgusting and… loose, but a better alternative to what he'd already endured.

He let out a heavy exertion as he dropped to his stiffened knees. They too buried themselves in the field of sloppy muck. Much to Dolly's amusement.

As Aaron gathered his senses, breath, and composure, he focused on something that distracted him, not too far out in the misted distance.

"Whatcha doin?" asked Dolly.

Aaron didn't even hear her. Instead, his eyes just adjusted as much as they could. They began to focus like the lens of a camera.

Dolly slung her hips back and dropped next to Aaron. She stared at the side of his tranced face, then followed the line of his vision. Her eyes widened and she shot right back to her feet and began to bounce with uncontrollable joy.

"Nior!" she shouted at the top of her lungs and waved eagerly at what she saw.

The shout pulled Aaron out of his state.

"What's a Nior?" he asked.

"That's my friend! My Horse!" She cleared her throat then forced a polished accent in a lower tone. "My noble steed!"

She giggled and danced while she burst at the seams with innocent happiness.

"I found you!"

"The horse is your friend? The one you lost?"

The love that sat on Dolly's expression answered his question. The whole time, Aaron had followed her blind, convinced the friend she'd lost was Rhian, out of some blind chase for hope. He wanted so bad to walk away, find his door, and exit - try another world. But instead, he forced himself to his feet.

"Let's go get your horse," he said.

Forty feet was the distance between them and the black stallion when Aaron was forced back from his stride by an invisible force. Uncertain of what happened, he retook the steps that were stolen from him, only to be met with the same, angry resistance.

He reached his hand, palm out, and it rested flat against the air. Like a camouflaged wall, it was solid and immovable.

To the eye, it seemed Aaron had just held his hand out to halt the universe, but in reality, the air it sat upon was as solid as steel.

"What the?" He turned to Dolly. He thought maybe she had an answer.

Just a few feet behind him, she stared at him. Her eyes didn't move. For the first time in their encounter, he saw the look of worry on her face. To hell with the invisible wall, he wanted to check on her.

"Hey," he said. "What's this all about? Where's my cheerful Dolly gone?"

Her bottom lip began to quiver.

Aaron, softly, and a little bit worried, rocked her shoulders back and to. He called her name twice before she snapped out of it.

"We can't go there." The cold breeze almost crystallized the water that began to form in her eyes.

The concern was a new spirit to what he'd become adjusted to. "Why, what is that?" Aaron asked.

"That's where they live," she said. Her eyes were glassed over.

Aaron glanced to the force that fought him, then back to Dolly.

"Where who live, Dolly? Help me out here. Who's *they*?"

It was a strange moment in a slow passage of time as Aaron suffocated in the new change of dynamic.

Dolly stood still and shook her head, so he repeated his questions until she answered.

"The memories." Her lips barely moved like they were frozen. Her eyes never blinked. Her face barely twitched as she said the words.

"Memories of what?"

Dolly beat around the bush so hard that all Aaron got, was that she didn't belong on this side of her world. He took it upon himself to try and break through the wall that resisted him. First, he threw a stone at it, the size of a grape, then leaned into the area it impacted. The only thing it did was push him back again.

The same ignorance replied to his every attempt. Sure enough, Aaron began to take it personally. His frustration led him to repeatedly punch and push at the barrier.

After a minute of his fight with the barrier, Dolly grabbed the back of Aaron's arm to stop him, but as she did, his arm slipped right on through like nothing was there. He pulled his arm back. Dolly let go. Aaron reached his arm out once more, only to be stopped again.

*Wait...*

"Hold my arm again."

She did. Aaron's reach pierced the barrier with no effort.

"Now let go."

His arm was spat out like unwanted food as she released him. It only confirmed what Aaron had tested.

"Dolly, I don't think I can go in there without you. You saw that, right?"

She laughed through the fear in her eyes, but Aaron saw right through it. He may have been out of his element, but he wasn't stupid. She'd called them memories, and only she could pass the barrier. Coupled with the fear in her eyes, it wasn't hard to narrow it all down.

"This is who you are, isn't it? Why you're so cheerful?"

His finger drew her attention over the far side where her horse stood. Miserable clouds, almost opaque in their blackness, drowned the foot of the castle in a vignette of doom as they moved around. The other side of the barrier that restrained them was a different atmosphere altogether.

"Those… what you called memories… they're memories of times where you… where *Rhian* had to pretend to be happy, aren't they?"

Dolly shivered a nod with stiff posture and eyes that refused to close.

"Every reason you ever had to act so… perfect, was because everything else was the opposite. Pretend everything's okay so everything *is* okay, right? I've seen it before. I don't know your situation… Rhian can't remember it, but out there, in the real world, you're like many others who wear a smile to hide the pain."

Nothing but the same, cold stare answered him as the wind began to pick up its pace and bit at Aaron's cheeks.

Dolly looked away. She didn't want a part of it. She knew the pep talk was going.

Softly, Aaron reminded her, "You don't have to be afraid, Dolly. Nior is right there, and he needs your help. Yours, not mine.

"All you have to do is take that strength I know you have and use it. I know you have it in you because I know who you're a part of. Ten says that wall's there because you're denying yourself…"

Aaron looked back to the eery clouds that circled the castle, like predators.

"Of the role they played in making you."

He held out his hand in the hope Dolly would do the same.

"You can do this. I'm right there with you."

After a battle with her fear, Dolly eventually, reluctantly reached for the hand of the man. After all, so far, he'd not given her any reason to doubt him.

Aaron held her, head against his chest, aimed at the floor in a paired hunch. Absolutely no resistance met them as they crossed the barrier and took steady steps, one at a time.

Halfway to Nior, a low-toned hiss filled the air. It unsettled them both. The shadowed blurs had moved and began to circle directly above them.

*If we keep our heads down, we're good,* Aaron thought, but Dolly had other ideas. She lifted to inspect the noise and jolted stiff as one of the tinted blurs passed through her. She shoved Aaron away with a violent extension of her arms. It was a monumental force for someone of her slender build.

Possessed, almost, her eyes glossed over in a smoked black tint. T-posed in her stance, stretched to her bodily limits, she was locked to the will of the darkness as the memories she'd locked away passed through her like ghosts.

From his tumble, Aaron pleaded, "Take control, Dolly. I know you can hear me."

Dolly began to spasm.

"You're pushing the darkness back... it's not healthy. Ember told me she has memories too; they made her feel like she didn't want to be here anymore. But she accepted them. Dolly, she used the good to *counter* the bad."

Dolly blinked. Like she heard him.

"Remember them as what *made you*, but don't forget who you *are*!"

Nior's neigh reigned over the pleas. The voice that reached out to her dangled in front of her like a carrot on a stick. Neither the neigh nor the kind voice would give up, not until it brought her back, and soon...

Dolly found reason to take a fight against her captor. Her arms yanked and pulled away from their locked position. Her legs shook. Her eyes jammed shut.

"Life's not worth living if it's not built, Dolly. Look at what you built. Remember my voice... remember the orchard, Nior, and the cottage. Remember our adventure. Please."

A tear broke free from Dolly's eyes as they shot open. The dark that once masked them, was gone. Deep inside her irises played the memories that Aaron recounted, like a slideshow of happiness: Aaron as he met her, the boots he passed her, the apples she'd picked. The wildlife. Everything.

The whites of her eyes fluxed into a luminous blue as she yelled out as far and wide as she could. When her scream reached its peak, the energy it carried exploded into an azure burst of mist. It floated for a moment, aimless before it found its target.

It reached out to the dark clouds that invaded the sky, one by one with a sharp grab and turned them the same shade of blue as it. It didn't last long, but as Dolly's energy engulfed them, they disappeared with little struggle, one with the air that hugged the world. The skies brightened and opened up. The snow and ice returned to a fine show of pleasant grass. It seemed like a timelapse to look at, as Aaron watched the snow beneath his feet melt away in an instant.

Dolly dropped slow to her delicate knees with a slight thud.

"Hey." Aaron ran forward and cupped her limp body into his shoulder. He hoped she was okay. "Talk to me."

Through exhaustion, she asked, "How'd you do that?"

"What?"

"That blue magic thing."

Aaron chuckled through his nose. "No, Dolly. That was all you. Watch."

He picked up a small stone from beside him and threw it where the barrier once held him back. The stone sailed through and landed ten yards past it.

"Free."

Dolly's face filled with glee. She bounced to her feet as if nothing had happened. She wondered if having let 'them' free, was bad for her.

"You can be as happy as you want to be. This is *your* home," Aaron reassured. "It doesn't matter what brought you into the world, good or bad. What matters, is who you are." He wiped the dirt and debris that made its way onto her lovely blue dress and followed her, finally, to her horse.

Clank! Went the chain as it bounced against the post that Nior was tied to. Now he was free to roam as before, and Dolly was ever so grateful.

"Oh, Nior," Dolly said. She loved him dearly. "I missed you so much! Please don't run away from me again."

As she stroked Nior's silky-smooth coat, an invasion of white light masked out everything. It could have burned eyes it was that bright. But, when it settled, Aaron and Dolly found themselves back at the cottage, with Nior in his stable. Home, as it should be. A return to how things were before like nothing had happened.

"I guess that's my cue to leave," said Aaron.

"Do you have to?" Dolly left Nior at the stable and stood with her head turned up to Aaron. She took the loose boots from her feet and passed them back to him with a gratuitous smile.

He signed. "I do. I'm sorry… I should have said it before. I came here to find Rhian, not Nior. Since she's not here, I have to go… try again, I'm sorry I lied." He pulled his boots over his muddied, damp socks.

Dolly pushed her hand against his back as he bent. "Oh, you didn't lie." She looked at Nior. "You found him with me!"

"Yeah, I guess I did." He winked at Nior as he stood. "At least I found something."

"Hey, don't beat yourself up, friend!" Dolly's shoulders shrugged high to her ears. "You'll find her. She's the best of us!"

"No," Aaron replied. "You're *all* the best. You're great in your own way, Dolly. I'm happy I met you, finally."

Dolly's cheeks got pretty hot all of a sudden. She turned her head away as she blushed.

"Can I ask you something?"

"Sure," said Dolly. "What's up?"

Aaron looked back, across the distance to the castle that peeked above everything. "That, back there… the memories. Is it just me or was all that just… a little convenient?"

A giggle answered him. "Why?" she asked.

"If I hadn't shown up, you'd never have taken that adventure with me, right? You'd have never found Nior… never gone through what you did…" he reeled off.

"Maybe I'm overthinking, but I can't help but feel like I was supposed to be here."

"Maybe you were."

The smile across from him triggered one of his own. How could he not smile back at someone so happy? Aaron figured Dolly wouldn't know the answers, so he wished her luck with everything and waved to Nior, who neighed back like he'd returned the goodbye.

"Bye!" She hugged him as tight as she did when they met. It was a quick hug, then she wandered back to the stable. The bounce in the steps she took, only she could pull off.

Done, Aaron began his journey back through the forest and back to his exit, but not without one last look before the cottage disappeared from his sight.

Dolly was in the orchard, basket in hand as she reached to the trees, and Nior was comfortable in his stable. The sun shone down like it deserved to and offered Dolly and her 'noble steed' the heaven-like glow they deserved.

At peace, Aaron ventured back to the door and through the white void that swallowed him, back to the building that sat on the island. He watched as the door closed behind him. Sure enough, it disappeared as it closed, and he'd left Dolly and her fantastic world behind. There was something about her cheerfulness that he just knew he wouldn't see twice. He'd miss that one.

Back in the room of doors, after a couple of test twists and some prayers, it was the dark green door that was unlocked. Aaron straightened himself out, took a breath, and opened it. He had no intention of wasting any time, and with that in mind, five steps in as many seconds were all it took for him to cross the threshold into yet another new world. One that would eat him alive…

# 5

## MA'AM

All of a sudden burdened with an unspeakable weight, the door took an almighty push before it sank back into its frame. A chunky steel door that weighed ten times the man who thrust his entire body weight against it.

With an echoed thud it closed, and Aaron, with all his strength, span the central wheel counterclockwise until it locked into place with a metallic clank.

Out of breath, he shook his wrists while he took in the view for the few fine seconds he found.

A mud-ridden, cobble coated, thin passageway leaked through cramped shrubbery. The sky above, grey with heavy, miserable clouds. He already missed the sun and the snow, mere seconds into the next world.

As he took a single step forward, three females, faces covered in thick black masks, pushed from the bushes around him. Two from the right, one from the left.

All three sported 1940s era pinks and greens, ripped and dirty. The two on his right held M1 Garand rifles, and the one on the left, an M1917 sniper with iron sights. All of which pointed at Aaron's head as they advanced. The women were very organized. Professional. They weren't there to play.

Aaron shot his arms up past his head in instant surrender. Scared, his mind ran circles as it wondered what he'd stumbled into.

Against his right shoulder, the bayonet of an M1 pushed. Its wielder urged him forward with a single flick of her head. He didn't want his head separated from his shoulders any time soon, so Aaron did as he was told and followed the slippery cobble path through the treeline and past the bushes.

He took a quick glance behind. The door was gone. It had disappeared into nothing but a mirror image of the very woodlands he traversed.

*Great, just perfect,* he thought.

The path came to an end, eventually. It opened up into a vista of worn khaki tents that positioned themselves above lines of trenches. Thin spots of rain started to trickle down and bounce off Aaron's already wet-with-sweat face.

The biggest tent, an operations tent, easily doubled the size of the others and had three entrances. They went through the main; the entrance that doubled the size of the others. Its material door was rolled up and held in place by thin black rope.

Inside, a woman stood at the back. She leaned over a collapsible metal table as she scanned a sizeable map. It was held down in each corner with a dirty rock.

She looked busy. Important. All Aaron could see was the back of the service hat that sat on top of her tied-back hair. The heavy boots she wore hugged into her shins, the grips at the bottom of which, were easily an inch thick. The black trench coat she wore draped down so far that it almost met the padded collar of them.

The three masked strangers pushed Aaron ahead, and his knee smacked sharply against the corner of a stray metal chair. It garnered a wince from him, but also the attention of the woman at the back.

As she turned, Aaron didn't know what to expect, but it sure wasn't the emblem that presented itself on the front of her hat; the face of a pink teddy bear, with one eye shaped into a cross.

Aaron figured it odd. Then again, at that point, everything already was.

The woman took a firm stance ahead of Aaron after a few stern steps forward with her hands linked behind her back. The three women around him lowered their weapons and took two steps of retreat.

The face the leader wore resembled Rhian's. For the third time. This one was Ma'am. She was a soldier, a leader. She and her mute trio were deep in a war that at the time, Aaron knew very little about. She was a survivor, the strongest of them all. Leader of the pack, and yet, her eyes showed a hint of burnout.

Aaron had disturbed their operation.

"What's the situation, then?" she scowled.

It was met with a slight groan from Aaron's throat as he struggled to piece together the words his mind had scrambled into oblivion.

"Swell," she said. "Must be out of your mind coming in here. Quite literally. Your name escapes me."

She snapped her fingers. "Remind me."

"A-Aaron. Aaron Haze. Sorry, we've met?"

The intimidating reflection of Rhian chuckled as she confirmed they'd previously met. She asked the 'chump' why he had sought to tamper with their mission.

As Aaron briefly remembered being called a chump once upon a time, by a personality whose name eluded him, he asked what he was supposed to call her.

The woman stood tall. "Call me Ma'am," she saluted.

"Ma'am it is. Quick question if I can?"

Ma'am exhaled. She didn't exactly have time for it, but allowed his question, just about.

"When we last met… on the surface, what led you up there?"

"Same thing as anyone else. Memories. Protection," she shrugged.

Aaron had heard that turn of phrase so often before. He raised his brows as his eyes jumped to the roof.

"You all say that you know, memories. But nobody ever really talks about it."

Ma'am lost her patience, not that she had any to begin with. She unlocked her hands and pushed against Aaron's shoulders, it him back a good step.

"If we wanted to gossip about it… if we *liked* to talk about it, none of us would be here, would we?" She orchestrated a circling finger in the direction of his eyes. "I can see how lost you are in them beady little lookers of yours… makes me wanna punch you in the kisser again."

The memory of Rhian's fist as it hurtled into the left side of his jaw thrashed over him like a tsunami.

"That was you? Damn." He shrunk down. Mentally, anyway, as he rubbed the side of his jaw and remembered the ache that particular punch left. He didn't want a second one.

"Listen, pal." Ma'am retreated to her table, she had more important things to do. She'd had enough of Aaron. Frankly, she had no intention of being anyone's babysitter.

"What is it you want? And do me a favour… get to the point. Don't be a wise guy about it."

For what felt like the hundredth time, Aaron reeled off the events that led him to Ma'am's world. From the nightly terrors to the blackout. Every time he had to explain it, it cut him deeper, and Ma'am could hear the agony in his voice as it pushed out a tremble.

With a calmer composure, Ma'am reached out to the sliver that was left of her mild-mannered side.

"Why didn't you just call Felix?" she asked. A light smile crossed her chapped lips. "He's an ace at this stuff."

Aaron had seen such a smile before. Ma'am was fond of Doctor Perkins. Through all the toil and trouble that he'd already experienced, Aaron knew just how difficult it would be to break the news. He closed his eyes, gathered his words.

"Felix… Doctor Perkins… Isn't around anymore."

"What'd you say, fathead?" she snapped.

"He's the first person I called," Aaron explained. He inhaled deeply. "The woman who answered said he'd passed on about a few months ago. I'm sorry, it sounds like you thought a lot of him."

91

Ma'am's head bowed to the floor with the slouch of her shoulders.

"I did... eventually. He had... the gift of the gab." As she picked her head back up through pride, she slipped a laugh through her nose. "First friend I ever made. Punched him as well, once."

Through the sound of rain as it danced off the canvas roof of the tent, and the gentle cracks of the thunder that began to approach, Ma'am looked at her right hand. It was laced with mud, dirt trapped beneath her bitten nails.

"Last time I saw Felix, I shook his hand. Poor bastard spent years of his life working for that... guess I caved at the right time."

Aaron, unseen by Ma'am, lit a soft smile on his face. It was nice to see that even Ma'am had someone she could call a friend. He felt her loss from across the length of the tent.

"I'm sorry," Aaron said. "I never got the chance to meet him, but I heard he was good with Rhian. The best, even."

Ma'am had no answers to give, and no snide remarks to mask what she felt. The news of the man she once knew left her to linger on fond memories as she clouded the world out and took it all in, one moment at a time.

Aaron gave her the peace she needed and pulled up the chair that once clapped against his knee. He waited, patient, and his gaze wandered around the tent. He recognised it from somewhere but couldn't put his finger on it. Even the map where Ma'am stood, held down by rocks, triggered something… but with everything that served to blend his mind into mush, he lost the connection he tried to decipher.

Time loitered. Minutes passed. The rain outside remained, but the clouds had lightened a shade.

Ma'am's grievance was shattered when from nowhere, obnoxious war sirens rang from all directions. The three women that stood in unison behind Aaron rushed from the tent in a scurry at the nod of Ma'am's head, and Aaron jumped from his seat.

"What's going on?" he demanded.

But Ma'am had no time to answer. She grabbed her rifle from its perched position against her map table and grabbed the green helmet that hung from its bayonet. She took a glance at Aaron.

"Stayin' or coming?"

Aaron wasn't going to stay. He clutched the helmet as Ma'am slung it sharp. It thudded against his chest. He watched, reddened with anxiety as Ma'am rushed from the tent, engrossed on the danger. He followed her but struggled to keep up.

Through the trenches they trod, hidden from everything but themselves. Aaron struggled to gather any form of grip as the mud they called the floor was tainted by rainwater.

In the maze, dizzy turns left and right seemed to never end, one after the other until Ma'am and her three followers hunkered down at one corner, lined with wooden planks. The corner they chose, diverted both left and right, but also sat directly opposite a mirrored opening. Then everything lit up.

Lightning flashed in the sky. A neon pink trace of electricity slashed through the vertical space between trench and cloud. It coated the environment with a surreal, blushed glow. As it cracked the sky open, it flooded a spotlight onto the warzone below. Hundreds if not thousands of enemy soldiers had begun to advance.

Aaron couldn't quite make them out through the distance and mist, but even still, it was enough to rattle his core.

Ma'am and her soldiers listed off a plan of action as they took cover at the corner. A precise, manufactured plan that sounded rehearsed. It felt *too* clean.

"Listen, you know how this goes. Keep it tucked - line to the left and wrap around. Three hundred yards on a dime, then take a right. Push the section, wait for the creepers to piss off then advance from the back, take them from the spine - hide 'em, then push 'til you're set on the marked zone, got it?"

A united nod from the three masked women. They cocked their weapons and awaited Ma'am's assertive count from three.

On her mark, they pushed their objective *exactly* as she told it, every letter, every syllable. Flawless. It all started with a crouched run.

Aaron watched; his eyes fixed as events unfolded. His mouth shrugged with the bob of his head; it was impressive. For a moment he thought he'd been sucked inside a movie. He scratched his temple with a single knuckle, then looked down as Ma'am watched and cheered her women on.

"How'd you know about the two soldiers there? What did you mean, 'you know how this goes,' you done this before?"

His questions were interrupted. An airhorn bellowed that dominated his and everyone else's ears. Aaron looked to the sky where it originated. A massive air balloon descended from a break in the clouds. It was pink... a nice pink. The kind of pink you'd find in a child girl's room, the same pink that coloured the emblem on Ma'am's hat. From its basket hung huge, mounted turrets that threatened the field. The balloon itself was easily a hundred feet from basket to tip.

*What the...*

"Now!" shouted Ma'am into the depths of the trenches, so loud it would have been impossible to not hear, regardless of distance.

In response, her soldiers jumped from their canyons, onto the field and unloaded their guns.

Aaron had to take a second look as the action played out. Pink lasers shot from the guns the women held. Real lasers, in the same neon pink as the lightning that drew scars upon the skies. They disintegrated every soldier they hit. For Aaron, it was another gaping step away from reality and into something… trippy.

Ma'am grabbed him by the scruff of his neck and dragged him through the zig-zag trenches just as a red rain of hellfire fell from the turrets beneath the balloon ship. They missed Aaron by a few feet at best.

Disoriented, Aaron patted himself down when he got the chance. Thankful to still be in one piece, but also in question of how he *was* still in one piece. His mind raced laps faster than Jimmie Johnson as it filled with a volatile mix of red and pink ordnance.

Ma'am dragged him deeper into the trenches before he could take it all in. A little further, then they stopped. She signalled him to hush with a single finger as two enemy soldiers walked past the crossing where they sat. A further inspection took the last uncompromised parts of Aaron's dwindled brain away from him.

Torn, ripped flesh exposed bones in their legs, arms, and jaw. Greyed skin stained with blood, rotten and blistered. They stank like death and snarled as they hobbled past. Both dead and alive at the same time, it was obvious what had walked past.

"Are- are those fucking zombies?!" Aaron asked in a forced whisper through gritted teeth and a stiff jaw. Maybe it was how cold it was, or maybe it was fear. Maybe it was both.

*Of course,* he thought. *Why not zombies, too?*

Ma'am had no intention of interacting with them. She waited, like she knew, then when a clearing opened, she took it and pushed through the cross-section.

In the clear on the other side, Ma'am took cover and counted to ten. At least, she tried to.

"What are you doing now?" Aaron asked.

Ma'am just clenched her lips and shook her head. Narrowed eyes frowned at Aaron as he messed up her count.

From somewhere unknown, a stick-like grenade flew into the muddy channel and bounced on the floor right next to them.

Through instinct, Aaron ran as fast as he could. But it wasn't fast enough.

Ma'am just stayed perched where she was. She lumped her head back until it bounced against the wall of the trench, and she sighed. A sigh so heavy it was clear above everything else.

"Here we go again," she muttered. A tinge of annoyance travelled through her words as the grenade exploded into a thick cloud of smoke and debris. It was violent and thunderous.

A flash of pink light blinded the field. Silence.

Aaron opened his tight-shut eyes and frantically threw his hands over his body in a rabid pat-down. He was… fine? But how?

He looked behind him. Three masked women, two steps back, with guns positioned at their side.

He looked to the front. A woman stood, leant over a table. A map below her eyes as she scanned it, its corners secured down by dirty rocks. Something Aaron had already seen, in perfect repetition.

*What the hell just happened?* he thought.

From across the tent, Ma'am let out a frustrated tut. She twisted her shoulders and head until they faced Aaron.

"Well, rookie," she said. "Got enough moxie in ya to go it again?"

# 6

## MA'AM: HERE WE GO AGAIN

A relentless whirlwind of panic and confusion ripped through the roots of Aaron's crumbled mind. It was enough to push him past his calm reserve and it became clear to him that he'd missed some vital information.

"Go it again?!" he snapped. Every breath he took held so much force they'd lift his chest and shoulders. "Is this a joke, is that what it is? Something's funny all of a sudden? What the *hell* was that?"

Ma'am knew she was in for a long conversation. She signalled the three unknown women to leave.

"No, I don't think so," Aaron insisted.

She liked it, did Ma'am, the new level of manliness that Aaron had started to show. A little bit would go a long way sometimes.

"Alright," she said. "Fair game. That… was attempt number… God, what are we at now? I've lost count, cards on the table."

It wasn't enough that she had no clear idea herself but to explain it all to somebody else seemed like an overly daunting task, even for her.

She sighed. "Mr Haze, I'm not exactly sure." She removed her stance in favour of a seat. She pulled it up a few feet ahead of Aaron. Much like him, she too, slouched on it.

"Took me a while to clock it, you know, pain in the ass. But, eventually, well… my best guess is we're missing something. Been on my mind for a while. Shit like that just…sticks."

Aaron's eyes lit up. "You need to finish."

Ma'am locked to him. The possibility of *finishing*… anything just felt so alien.

With a puzzle to solve, Aaron recalled his time with Dolly and wondered if maybe Ma'am, too, had hidden anything away, however small. Something that may have hidden a clue that could point them in a new direction.

Ma'am didn't wait about.

In the corner of the tent, lathered in jackets and helmets, sat a wide, six-drawer chest that practically fell apart at the joints. Ma'am removed the bottom drawer of the right side and carried it to the floor space between the chairs they had parked up. It broke the second it slapped the floor.

She rifled through its contents, disregarded junk to her left, and possibilities to her right.

Folded hats, handkerchiefs, medals, magazines, rusted knives, and a whole array of bullet casings.

*Hold on…*

Aaron snatched at the magazines Ma'am had discarded without question. He flicked through them one by one, and a particular one caught his eye. Slogans slapped all over the front that reminded him of times gone.

THE SISTERS THREE

MEET KATHY AND HER TRIO – THURSDAYS AT 9 PM

A BRAND-NEW TWIST ON SECOND WORLD WAR EVENTS!

"Kathy…" he muttered. Louder as he remembered the name, "Kathy."

"Yes?" Replied Ma'am.

Aaron brushed it off. "Oh, it's just the name of the--" Then it clicked. Like someone flicked a switch - realisation pounced on him. "Wait, your name is Kathy?"

"It is." Ma'am was straight-faced.

Aaron let a little chuckle slide through. "No… way…" It was like he'd met a childhood hero.

There was little time to discuss anything before the entire vicinity crumbled under the sound of sirens. They rang so loud they could have cracked eardrums.

Through the racket, Aaron made it as clear as he could that there was a chance he knew the answer, but he didn't plan on waiting about for the next repetition. As Ma'am began her march from the tent, weapon in hand, Aaron swiped the M1 before its withered butt even hit the floor. Like it was attached to it by a string, Ma'am's head followed the weapon without the slightest delay.

Aaron rested the barrel of it under his chin.

"What the hell are you doing?" Ma'am had more concern over the theft of her weapon than anything else. She *really* liked that gun.

Aaron rested his finger in an extended reach to the trigger down below. "It's a cycle, right? I think I know how to fix it. I'll… well I'll see you in a minute, I hope."

He clenched his eyes shut and pulled on the trigger. To him, the hope it wouldn't *kill* him lay strong, but if it meant a quicker resolve and an end to the madness, it was worth the risk.

A flash of white light sucked everything from existence – then he was back in the tent. He took a quick scan. Sisters three, present. Ma'am stood over her map, locked in concentration again. It was like he'd never left.

He paced forward, but not before he turned to the three masked women. His head beckoned them with a tilt, a sweet moment of role reversal.

"You three, too."

He'd already gotten Ma'am's attention from the moment he opened his eyes. She held a hunger for his little drama show to continue, and just knew he wanted the moment. Just like every cycle she'd ever witnessed, she remembered it.

"Go ahead, eager beaver," she said. "Stage is yours." She stood with her trio and watched as Aaron unfolded his self-proclaimed genius. She'd be the judge of that.

"Kathy," he said, randomly.

"Yes?"

"Just double-checking." Aaron pointed to the masked figures. "I'm assuming you're called the Sisters Three?"

They looked at each other, all three shrugged their shoulders at the same time.

Aaron ran to the drawer Ma'am had her trinkets in and pulled out the magazine he saw earlier. He presented it to the four women.

"Alright, so this is gonna sound really, *really* weird, but hear me out."

He pointed to the cover, three women stood in front of a tent, a fourth behind them, hands on her hips who looked important: their leader.

"This is a show that ran for a season in the nineties. I know because I used to watch it with my nan every Thursday night as a kid. This one…" He pointed to the main woman. "The main one… her name is Kathy."

Ma'am's interest peaked tenfold.

Aaron pointed to the other three on the cover, one by one. He took a brief pause over each. "These three, her soldiers, are called the Sisters Three. They're just like you three."

He looked to the trio. "Coincidence?"

"What does all this mean for us?" Ma'am asked.

Aaron cleared his throat. "It means I might have an answer. If you four… characters from a nineties show, are in here, Rhian must have watched it."

"That it?"

"No, Ma'am, that's not it. My guess is I don't think Rhian finished it. If she did, you four would remember. You carry the memories of it, after all, no?"

Ma'am nudged Aaron's arm with a loose fist. "You know, you're actually startin' to make a little sense here, cookie."

"Cookie?"

Ma'am shook her head with a laugh. "Don't worry about it. Carry on chief."

Aaron's neck cracked as he tilted side to side. He pointed to the far side of the tent. "Out there… what, we've got zombies, a gunship balloon thing, lasers, pink lightning… replace all that with Nazis, a Zeppelin, actual bullets, and miserable weather, what do you get?"

"Somethin' dreary," Ma'am quipped.

"You get the final episode. Bottleneck Bunker."

The blank look on Ma'am's face was priceless. She slipped into a steady state of confusion, only to be pulled from it with the snap of Aaron's fingers.

"You know what?"

Nothing.

"Ten says I know what you're supposed to do."

Ma'am wondered, "Ten what, exactly?"

"Don't worry about it, chief," Aaron remarked. "I'm sensing a pattern here." He swirled his hand above his head. "These worlds I've entered. You're all… I don't know, feels like I step into something every time… something that, God what am I saying? It all feels convenient."

Ma'am concentrated on Aaron's face. Her gaze dropped just an inch. Something ate away at her.

"To you," she said. "To us, this is a forever thing. Ain't nothing convenient about it."

"I didn't mean it that way." Aaron's words wouldn't slip out right. He hoped Ma'am would piece together what he tried to say. He waited for the sentence to form as he stared at the cover of the magazine.

"This. The Sisters Three. What are the chances that the first person to come in here from outside, has the information you've needed, in your own words, *forever*? To me, that means I *should* be here. I just don't know why yet."

Ma'am began to understand. When she looked at it from his perspective, anyway. She watched as the uncertainty in his eyes removed, and focus took its place.

He slung the magazine on top of a chair "Let's get to work," he said. "But first, can they take their masks off?"

The three stood and just looked at each other.

"Lay it all bare, as they say?"

Every face except Aaron's turned to Ma'am, who after a brief hesitation, agreed with a sigh.

The masked women co-operated and did just that. To Aaron's widened eyes, their appearance was something out of the ordinary. Each had the body of a human, but the head of a plush bear. A pink one to be exact. Pink teddy bear heads, each with their right eye crossed out. The same bear-shaped face that happened to be the insignia on Ma'am's cap.

Aaron was delighted. Of course, it had to get weirder. *Whatever*, at that point, there wasn't exactly a long list of things that would have surprised him, at least he thought.

"Okay," he said, and he laid out his plan, from his memory of the episode they were stuck in the cycle of.

He'd barely finished his account of events when the war sirens wailed again, and Aaron crossed his fingers in the hope it would be for the last time. As they sounded, all five of them looked at each other. It was now or never. Ma'am grabbed her weapon, but rather than leave ahead of the group, the sisters waited, and they all left together.

Same trenches, identical scenario, but this time a new team; a formation of five, and a new game plan. After one short huddle and ignorance to the previous approach they'd taken an infinite number of times, Ma'am, and her team instead, carried on straight through the bastard maze of trenches.

They bypassed their original hike to the right and escaped deeper than they thought possible into the field that surrounded them. Suddenly, it all felt bigger in scope.

By the time the obnoxious airhorn sounded its arrogant arrival, and the pink balloon descended from the sky, Ma'am and her squad were further away from danger than they'd ever been before. Enough distance that they felt safe.

A dead-end gave them sufficient cover at the end of the cavern they trod. Ma'am couldn't help but display her excitement. Funny, how giddy looked foreign on her, yet saddening, how it was the first time she'd felt true progress.

"Now we're cookin' with gas, kiddo!" she yelled through the warzone as it rampaged in full force.

Her body shook, but not from fear… from raw, uncontested adrenaline. She had it in spades. It was no surprise to anybody that Ma'am was ready for anything at a moment's notice. It switched on like a light.

Aaron peered his head above the ledge of the trench, like a brown-haired periscope, six inches for a glance. Masked by the thin mist of the clouds that fell, a bunker stood, just across the way. Solid yet blemished concrete that rose twelve feet from the uneven ground and housed two turrets. Two *big* turrets, they may as well have been cannons.

One of the three bear-faced allies gestured something to Ma'am. It was like sign language, one of the many languages Aaron didn't speak.

"What's she saying?" Aaron asked.

"The bastards in that bunker have no idea we're here." She pointed back to the trenches where her three brave soldiers would jump out on her mark. "Their eyes are on that, where we always go. We've got an edge."

A brief pause from Aaron, then he recited two lines from the tv show. It was a mutter, but everyone could hear him.

"We're never makin' it out this mess, the bunker's covered… not at the back it ain't Kathy… we gotta—"

He looked ahead. He pointed to the hill-mound that covered the rear of the bunker they'd scouted.

"We can flank them if we cover ourselves behind the hill. They're focused on the front, just like you said. They think you're in the trenches still."

"You son of a bitch, that's the money!" Ma'am slapped his head. "Flank 'n' burn… flank 'n' burn, girls!"

*Flank 'n' burn,* Aaron thought. *Just like Kathy used to say.*

Just off in the distance behind the hill-mound, he could spot a huge wave of zombies. They got closer and closer by the second. They had no time to waste.

"It's now or never, Ma'am. You wanna win this?"

"Hell yeah," she whispered with a smirk. It was game time. She stretched her hands to the ledge of the trench and pulled herself up. With a snarled grin, she and her team pushed.

It wasn't the quick show they had hoped for, neither was it a wide berth of danger, but within minutes they'd found their way around the risky flank, and in through the back of the bunker. They isolated the turrets from their mindless undead gunners and with them, rained down a storm of pink vengeance on the battlefield ahead until the barrels glowed red, and boy did they glow. Their brightness rivalled that of the lightning. It took hundreds of shots from each before they dwindled.

It all ended with a hiss as they overheated. The red turned to orange and the noise of the fight lessened. They'd turned half of the enemies that once gave them grief in the trenches, to dust. The sight ahead of them had become clearer than it had ever been, but it wasn't over, the ship still roamed the skies, and a horde closed in on them from behind.

"What now then?" Ma'am asked.

Aaron thought hard. "In the last act…" He peered from the cut-out in the bunker and tracked the balloon-shaped gunship of doom. "The Nazis retreated when the allied force blew up their Zeppelin."

Ma'am took a moment. She scanned the turrets up and down, then reached her hand underneath the barrel. With a hefty click, she'd un-lodged something.

"There you are," she said.

Then she felt around under the rotator mount. Another clunk and two pinch bolts fell from the turret. As it loosened, it shifted into a backward tilt.

"You stay here," she ordered Aaron. He was still oblivious to what exactly her plan was.

"Bit of help?" she asked her companions. They all rushed around the mounted gun, and with a quick three-count, they shunted it up until it separated from its mount.

Aaron couldn't help but fight a smile with pursed lips as he figured it out. Ma'am and the sisters shared the load and carted the heavy weapon out of the bunker over into the distance that masked them from Aaron's sight. Ma'am had a plan, a brilliant one, and the show was about to start.

From inside the bunker, Aaron wrapped his jumper cuffs over his hands as the air fought against his skin and kept watch, across the field, with a curious stare pointed right at the balloon.

Just as he predicted, with the faint sound of Ma'am's war cry in the background, a pink stream of concentrated fire shot across the sky, headed straight for the enemy's flying weapon.

First, it hit the basket and disabled a mounted gun. Then it hit the balloon itself but bounced right off of… whatever it was made of. Something strong enough to deflect lasers, apparently.

Finally, they hit the burners. As they ignited and reacted, the explosion that followed was magnificent. Like a mini-nuke had detonated in the skyline. The enemy ship veered in an uncontrollable downward spiral until it impacted the distant ground in a violent mass of flames and smoke.

Aaron stood by in wait. He expected everything that remained to just disappear… but instead, the zombies behind, and the sprinkle of undead left in front, all just… sprung into a little ball of pink confetti. Like a party cannon, but a little less… wholesome. One by one they burst out of existence until all that remained were

Aaron, and the four women who hoped they'd finished their mission. All fingers were crossed.

Later, at the tent, after everyone had settled, Ma'am was in the middle of a much deserved, welcomed celebratory toast. All hip flasks pointed to Aaron as he stood back, leaned against the tent doorway with a drink in hand, happy to just be in the moment.

Ma'am pointed her near-empty flask to Aaron.

"We may be from different worlds, us two, but credit where it's due, rookie, you're not all puppy dog eyes and questions. You got some steel about you there, somewhere."

Aaron nodded. Just a single nod. It was all that Ma'am needed. He drank the last drop of beer in the flask he held and placed at his feet.

It was pretty good - the taste of beer as it settled in his mouth, but before Aaron could set off on his next quest, Ma'am pulled him aside.

"Hey, where you off?"

"Oh, erm… I got—"

"Relax," she said. "I don't give a shit. What I mean is, you really just upping and running without so much as a goodbye?"

"Well, I guess not." Aaron lifted his head to the tent. "What will you all do now?"

It took a moment, but Ma'am got there. "Live, I suppose. Guess what happens next is written by us, right? Kinda' like it that way. Our way."

The sisters stood by at the tent entrance. They raised their hands to Aaron. He returned the farewell, regardless of how strange it still felt as he communicated with three pink bears.

As she watched it, Ma'am took a quick moment to grab something from inside her tent and rushed back with a gift. She held out a black mask to Aaron, one of the ones her sisters wore.

"Here," she said. "You might need this, depending on where you go next."

*A mask?* Aaron thought but swallowed the words on the tip of his tongue. "Thank you," he said.

"Gotta admit, I thought you were a drip. You're actually alright, keep it up," Ma'am winked. Then she held her hand out to his, and they shook. It was hard to tell whose shake was the firmest. Aaron was a little bit intimidated, again.

"Sure," he said. "Sorry that it had to be me to tell you about Felix. Would have been better coming from someone else."

"Nah, I'm glad you did. Proves you got some stones about ya. You're probably right too… about, you know."

Aaron didn't know. The day was… a long one. He raised his eyebrows and Ma'am read them loud and clear.

"The convenience. The 'maybe I'm here for a reason,' and all that. I hate to admit it, but… you helped me. Simple as that." She bumped her fist against his chest, twice. "A little help goes a long way. You take care, Aaron."

She felt weird as she called him Aaron.

"If it's better," he said. "Ember calls me Haze. It's grown on me."

Ma'am smiled as she ran the name in silence a few times. "Haze… not bad. Well alright then, take of yourself, Haze. I'll be seeing ya."

Aaron felt warm, as he saw Ma'am's happiness. She was free now. With a final goodbye and another competitive handshake, they parted ways and Aaron re-trod his dirty path to the door.

To his relief, the door was there, back just as he remembered it. No disappearing act, minus the one he himself was about to pull.

In the chaos, he'd forgotten just how unforgiving the weight of the door was. His feet dug in for grip, and with a little elbow grease, sure enough, it opened.

A few final steps saw him leave the warzone and back through the white void between worlds. Back to the room that housed the doors.

A quick wipe down of his soiled jumper. An even quicker stretch to rid the punishment his body endured. Aaron placed the mask Ma'am was nice to give him inside the slack of the pocket that sat on the rear of his jeans.

Maybe it was time to just... let off the gas and catch his breath. He'd earned a break, after all, however brief it would be.

# 7

## A MOMENT TO BREATHE

Aaron spun his eyes from his central stance. He took in the space around him again. From the tatty paint to the dull floors and the barred windows. His head threw a fit as it pulsed away. His separation from reality had dragged him down, and he needed a moment.

Once more he pushed at the heavy door hidden at the far end that divided inside from out and planted his feet in the stiff, shy grass. As the vapor poured from his mouth with every word he muttered, Aaron found the time to say what he had thought for a while.

"What the hell am I doing here?"

The bitter breeze felt nice. As it swept along his ears it served to cool that which burned. It helped the gears within his head slow their pace, long enough that he could breathe without being told he didn't belong there, or without an insult thrown into his face by someone whose face he loved.

Aaron was lost. He'd met three of them, yet through all the events that went to pass, and everything that was yet to come, he couldn't feel less involved. He couldn't feel more useless. He may as well have been stood in that living room again, looking down on Rhian as she lay there doing nothing. He felt as helpless on the inside as she looked on the outside.

He pulled at the slack of his jumper and cuddled into it with a locked back. It was filthy now. Disappointing; it was his favourite jumper. He didn't know if it was ruined now or if he'd wake up and it would still be clean. In fact, he knew very little about how this worked.

Aaron figured he'd earned the right to collect his sanity after running circles for infinity, almost literally in Ma'am's world.

He took a healthy amount of steps until he neared the lonely dock and picked up a smooth flat pebble that sat just inches from his rested feet. He clocked his arm back with a tilt and swivel of his shoulder, stared across the waters and let it rip.

Like a bat out of hell, the stone shot from his loose grip and skipped the moment it touched the water. Aaron counted five skips before it disappeared behind the blanket of mist, and then three more before he was met with silence. A silence that didn't seem to last long...

A gradual rumble presented itself below Aaron's feet. Like the tiniest earthquake. His ears knew it; it came from beyond the lake and far into the distance, but much like his first arrival, all he could see when he looked afar, was the white clouds that fell down, and a tall, dark building that poked its head shyly between them.

Maybe his head was messing with him, but that tremor felt awfully real. The dock was a one-hit-wonder now; it had nothing left to give. The stone was slung, it skipped away, now Aaron was bored. As a result, he understood what his mother used to say: only in boredom can you find new details in that which you think you know.

He'd never before noticed how the dock leaned at an angle slightly to the left, or how it rocked itself to sleep with every soft shift in the water. Until now, he'd not seen that the body of water reached around the building like the widest moat. What's more, Aaron was embarrassed how he'd never noticed that the building

118

itself, which was home to the doors, was cladded on the exterior. It was the little details that met him, but was it this way before? His mind was sent adrift as he tried to remember, but since he'd never taken it all in, he was only fed silence.

Aaron was the kind of guy who, much like many others, would lose himself in his moments of tranquillity... almost overstay his welcome when it came time to kick his feet back. And much like everyone else he knew; he always found the peace to be over too soon.

It was a feeling that remained the same when Aaron's exploration brought him full circle back to the dock as he roamed. One swooping walk, and he'd lapped the island. Trees sat opposite the water for the most part, until a gap appeared, and then there he was, stood with a long stare back into the foggy waters he'd not long skipped a rock on. Almost in the blink of an eye.

With the short supplies of activities that surrounded him, Aaron made his way back inside.

The first thing he checked was for signs of a door. Less the three that remained and more the one that brought him to the island in general.

He peered his head around the far corner as he walked inside. The first corner he turned when he arrived. Past the doors that remained, in an exact reversal of his entry. There was nothing. A plain wall that just mirrored the room around him, only it was swallowed in shadow and darkness as the walls that joined it cast their shadows.

Aaron sulked his head for a moment. It was worth a shot. So instead, he elected to sit from his stand, and just… meditate almost. Parked on the floor for as long as it took. Legs and arms folded. Eyes shut. Nothing but complete silence.

Not even Aaron himself knew how long he sat at that corner. It was long enough that his legs had to adjust when they stood back up. Also, long enough that they were riddled with a sharp static that so gracefully offered him a limp as he took a final glance from the barred windows.

With nothing to offer him, Aaron figured it was time to grab at some handles again. It was either that or mope for a while longer and just delay the inevitable.

Thankfully, this time the first door he tried was the one that was open. The yellow one. In the knowledge that his little break would have only extended how long this reality-bending quasi nightmare would take, Aaron decided there was no time like the present and walked on through.

Little did he expect just exactly what this door had in store for him.

# 8

## LITTLEFOOT

As tall as Aaron himself were the blades of grass that immediately welcomed him, and as wide as standing railway sleepers. Between them, the uneven ground shifted high and low, which made for a tricky sense of balance. If that wasn't enough, perfectly rounded pebbles were scattered throughout, only the pebbles were the size of boulders in the world in which he'd stepped.

*Okay*...Thought Aaron as he manoeuvred his body around the towering grass. He twisted and contorted his body in all directions just to push ahead, almost like a bloated obstacle course. It took *much* longer than he'd have liked.

But he came to a clearing, in time, right beside a one storey building. Practically right next to it he stood, yet at the same time, hundreds of yards away as every inch was the size of a stretched footstep.

As he snooped around and edged closer through the clumps of turned up mud that stood as high as his knees, he couldn't help but notice the far side of the building was scarred by fire. Dressed on the outside with black smears of char, like powdered paint.

He closed in on the behemoth of a doorway. It was slightly cracked open, but more than enough to fit his tiny body through. He thought it over. Should he go inside?

But from nothing, the area that surrounded him plummeted into a pool of darkness, like someone turned out the lights. The darkness itself was met with a biting wind. Short of ideas what could have caused it, Aaron slowly turned his head half a circle. A pigeon stood before him… but it was enormous.

Like Godzilla would lurk the streets of Tokyo, the bird loomed tall over Aaron. A monster. Easily ten times the size of him. The top of its pink tainted ankles reached his head as he stared at it in terror. His head anchored all the way back just to get a good look, and the bird cooed. It rumbled the air like a soft thunder and curled up the hairs that sat on the back of the man's neck.

"Oh, hell no!" Aaron bolted straight for the door of the building in the search for shelter.

The pigeon tried to make chase with a couple of lousy pecks that dug craters into the ground like a gigantic hammer, but thankfully, Aaron was just too quick.

Inside the building, despite the ash and charcoal that lined the exterior, every room he saw looked lived in. Almost.

The fibres of the dirty, stained carpet in what looked like the world's largest hallway stood at attention to Aaron's shins as he waded through, like a walk through a shallow pool. Nothing could distract him from the stench that took refuge in his nose. Cigarettes and feet. Lovely. It was a smell so strong he'd already forgotten about the pigeon.

Broken pieces of glass lay throughout the carpet. To Aaron, they were the size of dustbins. Not to mention the disgusting, crumpled up cigarette ends that sat as big as him in comparison, right next to fallen columns of ash. The whole scene looked like a junkyard.

It didn't sit well with him that he'd been reduced to the equivalent size of his own thumb, and as he struggled through what felt like miles of carpet, he slapped low and kicked high at it in what he believed was a much-deserved childish grump.

"Stupid," he remarked. "Yeah, let's throw him into a world filled with lava... he'll have a laugh."

Then he kicked a stray-laying fag butt square in the filter. It almost broke his foot.

"How about a fairy-tale land? No? Zombies and lasers?"

He grumbled and groaned. "Actually, I'm alright with the lasers."

He took a sharp inhale through his nose. "Even better, how about some Thumbelina, Alice in Wonderland, Honey I Shrunk the kids mess? He'll love that!"

He thought he was being punished, but of course, didn't know why. He lifted his feet with a big stride to pass over a shallow ridge as carpet changed to solid ground under another skyscraper of a doorway.

He stood on a cream-tiled floor that was plastered with filth. The texture was that pronounced it could have been mistaken for a common cobbled street, and the grout lines, thick with muck as they were, were easily a foot deep to him. Aaron had seen some dirty floors before, but this one was something else.

Navigation was definitely easier, but Aaron was soon stopped in his tracks by a thud that shook the ground and threw his organs to the blender. Then a tense five seconds of nothing before another trembled the floor. Again. And again, until the sound and vibration matched the entrance of a colossal foot as it crossed from the leftmost doorway. The foot was so large, Aaron's waist would have met the sole of it.

He wasn't going to just stand there and get stepped on, so Aaron darted for the nearest cover he could find: a table leg half a marathon from where he stood.

The little legs that paced made it to the wooden leg, that stood sixty feet taller than him, at least. The table that it met, canvassed above Aaron like a massive, deserted warehouse. One with a floor that had never seen a mop.

Aaron watched as the giant feet ventured to and rested by the sink, the water that gushed made it apparent he had the time he needed to escape. As he moved, he saw most of the giant figure that sported the supersized boots. A male, denim jeans and a dirty white vest. Everything else from there up was drowned in darkness. Air rattled through his ears as the man groaned… something.

As he wiped the beads of sweat that sat motionless on his forehead with his jumper that was now only good for the bin, he left the room with haste through the door the man came from.

In the exploration, he passed things he wouldn't dream of talking about, like a syringe. Just aloof among the floor without a care, so big he could probably sleep inside it like a cryo-chamber. He dreaded the thought of what was inside it.

It was quite the walk to get to the unmistakable bedroom, but he made it and passed the broken white door on his way in.

To his horror, it was a child's bedroom. Centre-place on the wall sat a sticker of a pink hot air balloon. It sat directly above a single bed, sheeted with the same shade of pink, only stained like they'd never been inside a washing machine. Ever.

Across from the foot of the bed, an old tv. Aaron thought back to when he was a child; he had a similar one in his room. Technology had come a long way since those big backed, too heavy for their own good telly's.

The glass on the front of this tv was cracked like something had been thrown at it. It sat on a flimsy, narrow chest of drawers, the handles of which were mostly broken. Down, lined up below the drawers, on the floor were three pink teddy bears. Each with an eye crossed out in its design.

Aside from the drawers, tv and bed, the room lay bare. Stains and ripped paper rode the walls and mould grew in the seams of curtainless windows. The light that seeped in only highlighted the dark bloodstains on the carpet. Different shades like they'd tainted it at different times.

It took a second glance at the blood, the bears, and the picture for Aaron's heart to collapse inside his chest. With it went his shoulders, as low as they could drop.

"This was your room, wasn't it," he whispered through a tightened throat.

Until that moment, he had no scope of Rhian's childhood. That which she remembered - she never spoke about, and the quantity that she did know, was very little. However, the room he stood in started to paint a very clear picture.

With a lack of want to stick around, Aaron took a hike to the next room. It sat right across the hall. Usually a few small steps, but in this world, an entire field trip.

He freed himself from the depths of the carpet as he crossed the hall, and onto a bare concrete floor. There was a bit of a wrestle to get around the bumps and grooves it produced.

Careful of his foot placement, Aaron shot under the ten-foot gap of the sofa right of him when he noticed the two giants that sat on it: the white tank-top wearing man, and an overweight woman in a red shirt of sorts. Their faces were drowned in shadow, but Aaron ran far too fast to cover, to see them anyway.

The breaths that cycled in and out of the man who hid, resembled a panic attack. A big one.

"Shhhh," whispered a voice from far into the corner, within the depths of the dark. It startled Aaron even more.

He followed the sound as far back as he could, until, unveiled by the smallest crack of light that snuck down behind the seat, he saw her.

Her white jeans stood out the most, as did the dungaree straps that mounted her shoulders. For a second, it looked like they were floating, but then Aaron saw the baby-blue t-shirt that sat upon the woman who hunkered against the far leg of the sofa.

Immediately, he recognised the posture. Back pushed up against a hard surface, and hands that protected her head. She looked like she was constantly trying to escape something.

"Littlefoot?" He asked in a hushed, tender tone.

The fragile woman glanced up, and their eyes met. Hers widened as she got to her knees, crawled over with a scrape of her brittle white shoes, and hugged him. She was so happy to see him.

"Have you come to free me?" she asked as her pig-tailed hair burrowed into Aaron's chest.

*Again?* He thought. But he chose to reciprocate Littlefoot's embrace with his own, happy to be safe from what he'd perceived as a realm of chaos.

"It's okay," he said, softly.

Littlefoot finally let him go. "How are you here… with me?"

"Honestly, it's a really a long story. Have you seen Rhian? Don't know where she is do you?" He asked, locked on to a face that mirrored the one he was looking for.

Littlefoot was quick to respond. Rhian would never have crossed into her world. Her head shook softly as it bowed down.

Aaron knew deep down the only answer he would have got, would have been the one he did. It didn't make it any easier. He sensed a running theme within the doors of the island, and rather than wait for the inevitable, he asked, "Do you need my help?"

Her once shake turned to a nod. A shy nod. With little hesitation, Aaron asked where they should start.

She wanted to leave but she was too scared, the giants on the couch above her constantly frightened her stiff. It was understandable, it scared Aaron, too.

Aaron just wanted it all to be over. If he freed her from the hiding, he could leave, right? With just that thought alone, he quickly took her head in shelter against his chest, left from underneath their cover and retraced his steps with caution until they were both outside, where the wind flirted with their hair.

*Job done,* Aaron thought. *Nice and quick.*

Beneath the overhang of the door ledge, they stood. The gap between it and the floor was more than enough, considering their scale. One single flaked piece of paint drooped down like an awning. It was sufficient for a moment, as they spoke.

The look of wonder and awe on Littlefoot's face spoke volumes. Curious, Aaron took the time to ask why she'd never thought to 'just do that,' before.

"I've tried," she said. "But everything… is just so… dangerous."

"So why leave now?"

"You make me feel safe. You're always – You're nice to me."

Aaron shared with her a warm smile as the breeze flicked his greasy fringe. Strands of it had started to stick to his forehead in the mix of sweat and dirt.

"I always will be," he said as he looked around. He left his stare hanging toward the direction he'd entered from.

Littlefoot sensed his want to leave, and it gnawed away at her like a leech. As she always did, through habit, she bit her nails.

She asked, "You're not staying, are you?"

# 9

## LITTLEFOOT'S COURAGE

If there was one thing Aaron knew, it was that he hated to see Rhian upset, especially over something he'd said or done. He found himself in that exact situation as he looked at Littlefoot, and watched tears begin construction in her beautiful blue eyes. It crushed him.

"Hey," he said as he reached his left hand to her shoulder. "I promise I'll stay as long as it takes to make you feel safer. I won't leave until I know you're in a better place."

He meant it, too, through every fibre of his being. Any thought of the next door was pushed to the back of his mind as he leaned his head just a little closer and extended the smallest finger of his right hand.

"Pinkie promise?"

Littlefoot answered the shake. It was cemented now, and his words were magic to her ears. Finally, she had something in her world she wasn't afraid of. Something that promised her help. To Littlefoot, a pinkie promise was as definitive as a promise got.

Aaron knew he'd said the right thing just to look at her. He gazed outward, onto the vast land that presented itself before them. Like Ember's, it was another world that trod the lines of both beautiful and intimidating.

As Littlefoot watched, Aaron approached and climbed the best he could, the stalk of a weed that poked its head above the grassy lands. Flimsy as it was at the top, it supported him long enough that he could see far into the distance.

Trees, garden flower beds and rockery displays, fences. A sight to behold, and that he did. He absorbed the view for as long as he could. Then, with a grunt and a rough landing, he bent the weed with his weight until it would bend no more and dismounted. He gathered himself back with Littlefoot, who still wondered what his plan was.

"Okay," he said, still out of breath. "I think I have an idea, fancy a walk?"

With a dash of question and a sprinkle of joy, Littlefoot nodded. "Sure," and they set off. Neither of them really had an exact idea where they were headed, but Aaron maintained the illusion that his 'idea' might just work.

Through miles and miles of grass they wandered… all the way to the bottom of the garden.

Littlefoot felt safe next to Aaron. It wasn't because he gave the impression of an action hero, because he didn't. It wasn't through any impressive confidence he'd shown because -- he also didn't. But it was because unlike anyone else she'd ever met… he shared the scale of her world *with* her.

All around them, everything towered above them. They may as well have been traipsing through a city block in central New York.

Like a child's first time at a theme park, Littlefoot's eyes lit up with everything she saw. They widened so far it was like someone held them open. Surreal to Aaron, and wonderful to Littlefoot.

Even the insects stood tall as they strolled on past. They minded their own business as the pair of wanderers journeyed through. Ants carried leaves and droplets of water the size of footballs. Worms burrowed holes the size of traffic tunnels. Butterflies floated above them with a wingspan that drowned out the sun in glorious fashion. The wind the wings pushed fluttered the pigtailed hair that swung back and forth with every step Littlefoot took.

A world she believed heart and soul would eat her alive, had welcomed her. And it welcomed her with a big, bold display.

*This is amazing,* she wanted to say, but words eluded her open jaw. She just plodded on along, convinced she had fallen asleep and drifted into a dream world. The only thing stronger than her dream state was the hope that the safety she felt was real.

A few short hours later, Aaron and Littlefoot approached the base of a tree so large to them, it was beyond comprehension. It sat at the far end of the garden and towered over everything else in sight.

To the average person, it would have been one of the biggest common trees they'd ever seen, so to them, who stood just above an inch tall, it was a sight to behold. It sat right beside a gentle, narrow stream.

A crack that formed between two conjoined roots as they straddled above the dirt, opened into a gap that hollowed out the inside of the tree, like a huge, elaborate doorway. It may as well have had a welcome mat at its entrance. They walked inside it, past a pile of leaves and twigs.

The mid-afternoon sun peeked through gaps and cracks within the tree and shared its radiant warm glow. It made it feel comfortable and homely. Exactly what Aaron had hoped.

Aaron's eyes met Littlefoot's. "What do you see?"

Littlefoot scanned around for a while. Every inch of the space. It was like a massive, empty room that carried a small echo whenever they made even the slightest noise.

"Nothing," she said.

"Exactly. Now imagine a kitchen – do you eat?"

Littlefoot laughed and rocked her head left to right. "No, what's that?"

Aaron's eyes narrowed. He looked at his own stomach, then back to Littlefoot. Then another look to his stomach. He was still mid-adjustment to how all the different worlds worked, nothing seemed to be consistent outside of the faces he saw.

"So, how do - when…" He rattled his head quick and sharp, then exaggerated a blink. "Never mind," he said. "What *do* you need?"

The best question – no, the *biggest* question Littlefoot had ever been asked. What did _she_ need?

A bed, first and foremost. The long walk had tired her legs and her feet were sore, no thanks to her thin-fitted shoes. She remembered that she passed some twigs and plants on her way inside, maybe they could be of some use.

Aaron followed her as she dug into her find. Only the best, most comfortable looking leaves were considered. It was almost too good to be true just how well it all would work.

*What a find,* Aaron thought. His mind was on par with Littlefoot's. Everything seemed to work out wonders. Seemed.

In a split second, a bird swooped down from a branch of the tree and flew just inches above their heads. The gust it brewed was so forceful it knocked them both to the ground.

The bird just stood over the pile of twigs and leaves to defend what it had collected for its nest. Nobody was about to get past it.

Aaron dusted off his knees as he rose. He stood in a protective stance over Littlefoot. She knelt, head and body twisted away from the bird, and her hands protected her head in a frightened cower; the trademark Littlefoot position.

He thought and he thought as the bird's head danced around. Its eyes never left him. He didn't have much time. To the left of the bird lay a stick. Thick enough that it could deal some damage, while at a glance, big enough that Aaron could wield it.

A look back to the woman as she cowered, another to the bird… then the stick. Another idea had come to Aaron, but even he wasn't sure if it would work in his favour. Or if he even wanted to do it.

As he stared the bird down, he called to Littlefoot.

With a gulp, he said, "You remember that promise I made?"

"Mmhmm" Fear had pushed her head deep into troubled water. She found it impossible to use her words.

"When I say, you run. Run past me and over to that stream. Wait for me there, okay? Wait as long as it takes."

He geared himself into a ready position; Right foot back a step, body bent down at an angle ahead of his left.

"Ready…" The word lingered as Aaron second-guessed what he was about to do.

His right hand touched the ground, the toes of his left foot dug a little deeper into the mud until it slid an inch.

"Now!"

Aaron pushed his readied left foot as hard as he could into the ground. It shot his body forward like a bullet. A pace so fast the bird barely had time to react. It started to open its wings, and Aaron opened his arms and launched his body through the air with a jump bigger than any he'd made before. He collided with the top of the bird's leg as he grasped it. It sent both him and it into a violent crash onto the floor.

As the bird flicked its wings into the ground, in a struggled attempt to get back up, Littlefoot ran past in a blur. She'd never moved so fast.

Aaron ran for the stick he'd eyed up after he clambered to his feet. It sat in his hands like a bloated hockey stick. The unexpected weight of it forced him into a firmer grip.

Then the bird got back to its feet, but Aaron was ready. As it charged him, it chose to skip the odd foot forward in favour of a jump. Aaron raised the stick. As high as he could, and with tight-shut eyes, and a prayer for his life, he slammed it down. A might so hard it thrust his hips back and then...

Clang! The sound of metal reverbed through the air. A vibration shot down the bat so sharp it flicked Aaron's elbows out.

"Huh?"

Aaron opened his eyes. The stick he held was rested at an upward angle, between the thick metal bars of a cage that had imprisoned the protective bird from nowhere.

"Where the..." Aaron shifted his gaze to his right, where Littlefoot was standing. Tears streamed down her reddened face, and her hands were glued to the sides of her head.

Stuck for words, Aaron let go of the weapon. It thumped against the ground as it bounced at his feet. "Was that you?" He asked as he approached Littlefoot.

He pointed to the cage. "That thing?"

Littlefoot's eyes shot to the floor. She removed the grasp from her head and played with her fingers. "I… I don't know," she said.

"Littlefoot, was that you?"

The smile that framed Aaron's words confused her. His words themselves begged for a response, but she didn't know if he'd stay by her side if she told him what he appeared to want to hear.

Aaron cupped his hand around the back of her arm softly.

"Hey." His voice was softer than ever. "It's okay. Was that you… somehow?"

Littlefoot pushed out a breath that lasted the length of four and looked him in the eyes.

"I think so… I… I saw it all happening and heard the noise. I wanted it to – I shouted for it to stop but nobody heard me, so I imagined the bird was in a cage and then…" She looked at the trapped bird. "That happened."

Aaron sighed. But not from annoyance. He signed through the grin that separated his stiff lips.

"Well, that… changes things." He wiped the tear that sat alone above her cheek. "Come on, let's get out of here."

Far away from the tree and the bungalow, the sun had set, and the warm rays were replaced with cool beams of minted blue as the moon lit up the world.

Aaron and Littlefoot had walked aimlessly for so long that their feet began to blister, so, at the bottom of a steep stack of rocks, they sat. They took in the view that looked vastly different under the moonlight, and they just talked.

"Can I ask you a question?" Aaron took his boots off for a moment, as Littlefoot did with her thin canvas shoes. The night air soothed their feet with every pass. It was nature's bandage.

"That... back there. What actually was it? Do you remember how you did it or?"

Littlefoot shrugged her lips and sunk her shoulders. "I don't know. I just *thought* it and then, well, it happened I guess."

"What were you feeling?"

"Scared. I was angry too," she shivered.

"At the bird?" Aaron removed his jumper from over his black shirt and placed it around her shoulders. She clutched into it and sunk a little more. It was soft... and warm.

"At everything," she said.

Aaron recognised the lost look in her eyes as one he'd held in his own quite often during his journey. He picked up her shoes and began to wipe the dirt from them with his hands.

"I don't really know much about…" He looked around. "This place. Just what I saw on the way in. But I do know a little something about feeling lost in the world around you."

He slapped her shoes against the rock he sat on and knocked the bits of mud from the grips. Then he sat them down in front of her. It spawned the softest smile on her face. He was so nice to her.

"When I got here, the first world I ended up in was Ember's one. I felt so… out of place. Then I was in Dolly's land, and it happened again because it was so different. So… happy. A happy I'd never seen before."

Littlefoot leaned her head into Aaron's shoulder as he told his story.

"Ma'am's was the strangest. Still getting my head around that one… might even need therapy… *but* I guess what I'm saying is every world around you is a stranger until you accept it. That, I do know."

He turned his head down to meet Littlefoot's. She looked comfortable. She looked peaceful.

"I know yours scares you," he said. "And I know nothing can change that. But even if we can find you the littlest space to call your own, where you don't have to hide. I'd bet ten that this world of yours will feel a little bit safer."

He looked deep into the night sky and sighed.

"I just wish I knew where that was."

The tranquil minutes that floated by were bathed in a luminescence that drifted inch by inch until it met the garden rockery by which they were sat. To them, it was a mountain, to the world outside, just a decorative section of the garden that stood a few feet tall.

But as the beams of moonlight struck it, Aaron noticed the breach it highlighted between two of the topmost rocks.

*I wonder if...* He patted Littlefoot's shoulder and urged her to put her 'feet on.'

The canvas of her shoes slid over the small blisters on her bony feet. She passed Aaron his jumper back.

Aaron looked up to the climb they were about to make, then returned it back to her.

"It's gonna get a little colder yet," he whispered with a wink.

Little by little, step by step, they made it up the incline of rocks. In everyday terms, they'd scaled the height of a three-storey house. In reality, they were two feet off the ground.

As the rocks the size of caravans stacked up beneath them, Aaron and Littlefoot stood at the lip of one that neared the top. Behind them, was a gap between two more, big enough to park a bus. Big enough for Littlefoot to call home.

Kept warm by the ring of solar lights that surrounded the display, Littlefoot loved it. Something about it just offered a serenity that she'd never before experienced. But it was bare; she couldn't *live* there.

"It's empty," she said. Her head lowered.

Aaron knew, but he also knew something else.

"Littlefoot, remember the bird? The cage?"

"Yeah?"

Aaron stood ahead of her, he looked directly at her. She felt forced to look back at him.

He tilted his head to meet the angle of hers.

"That came from within you. You thought it – it happened. Maybe you can do that again."

"You don't know that though," she said.

But Aaron did, in a way.

"You remember I told you about the other places I'd visited?"

Littlefoot nodded.

"Well, Ma'am didn't know how her mission ended. Stuck in a loop – her mind didn't give her freedom. Then with some help, she finished it—"

"Your help, right?" Littlefoot asked.

"Yeah… I guess. More… direction. Just enough to break a loop. But now she can live how she wants… with control of it.

Ember remembers all the dark things that made her, so her world is built on those – of fire.

Dolly fought so hard to keep her memories locked away that they fought back and messed with her."

Littlefoot took a step back. "What does that mean for me?"

"It means, your world is connected to your mind, from what I can tell."

"My mind," she asked. She felt like she had no control over anything.

"I felt what you feel when I walked in here. I felt small, insignificant. I saw the building… the people… you. You sat there scared. But when I was in danger, you changed all of that and saved me. Just by imagining it."

Littlefoot looked down. Her eyes slowly tracked the floor from left to right. Aaron could almost hear her thoughts.

"Now imagine a place where you can sleep. Where you can be free from hiding under the gap of that sofa. Where you can feel a little less scared and a lot more in control."

He took a step forward and placed his hands on Littlefoot's shoulders. He looked deep into her soul.

"I thought you lot all connected because you look like her. I was wrong. You share something else."

He lifted a hand, placed a finger against her temple and tapped it. He didn't have to say anything.

"Okay," said Littlefoot. "So, what do I do?"

Aaron, a little uncertain yet somewhat confident, said, "Think of a home. A *you* home. You never have to go back to that bungalow again."

"How?"

"Just think of it. Hard."

He removed himself from in front of her, and elected to stand behind her, and watch the magic unfold with keen eyes.

Littlefoot stole a glance into the distance that revealed itself in the corner of her eye. Far north-west of where she stood. A final glance at the building she feared and hated yet knew so well. Then she took seven small steps until she was stood inside the roomy gap and all she could see was the emptiness within.

She closed her eyes, as tight as she could. She took a breath so deep it inflated and flexed her ribs, and she thought. She pictured a bedroom in the moonlight, a breeze that would run through her hair as she sat and watched her own tv. Everything she wanted so bad, just floated right there behind her eyelids.

"Aargh, I just can't do it!" Littlefoot cried after endless attempts to conjure a slice of happiness. She sulked down onto her knees. They hit the stone floor hard. "Why can't I do it?"

Aaron would have answered if he had one to give. Short of a reply, he knelt down beside her and held his hand to hers. He held it there until she coupled hers with it.

"Now try again," he urged. "But this time, don't think about needing it. Think about how bad you *want* it.

How much you deserve it. Focus on how you felt under that sofa and realise how nobody deserves that."

Littlefoot forced her eyes closed again. She tried so hard to remember and to think.

Aaron whispered, "Remember how *you* saved *me*. From the bird."

She took a deep breath through Aaron's words. To follow her through faith, he too, closed his eyes.

"And remember who you are. You're not just part of the strongest person I know, you're Littlefoot. Just as strong on your own, and you deserve everything." Littlefoot began to whimper, fully focused on the most important moment of her existence so far.

Aaron peeked his eyes open amid her strenuous groans. Then they widened.

A single, metal frame bed, complete with mattress and pink sheets – three pink bears lined the pillow. The sticker of a hot air balloon, a pink one, beside the bed on the wall of the rock. A cream shaggy rug on the floor. Drawers and a television. A bedroom. A perfect replica of the one Aaron found himself in earlier that day, only as it should be…clean. Bright and colourful. Perfect.

He whispered, "You did it." But Littlefoot didn't hear. She'd blocked the world out so well her ears followed suit.

He gently nudged her as she sat, fully focused next to him. The look of love that cast from her eyes as she opened them was unmatchable. Quick to her feet, she sprung into action and headed for the bed. She prodded it then flinched. She prodded it again, only this time with a full hand as it sunk into the mattress. It was soft. And what was odd to her… it felt real.

She did the same with the bears, one at a time. She looked around. It *was* real. She sat on the bed. It held her there in a soft cradle, and she spawned tears, only they were happy tears. She didn't mind those ones.

Aaron sat beside her, and she hugged him. So tight that he struggled to inhale his next few breaths, but he let the hug happen for as long as she needed it.

"See," he said through clamped breath. "I said you could do it."

The grateful woman released her vice-like embrace from Aaron's chest. Just as she hoped, he'd kept his word.

"You're not like the rest." She wiped the tears of elation from her rosy cheeks.

"The rest?" Aaron asked.

"Any of them. They always pity me… treat me like a child. You don't."

"You're not a child," he said with his eyes.

Littlefoot looked around at everything she was still trying to process. "I feel safe here."

As the words left her mouth, white light filled the newly occupied room, and as it calmed, a door appeared at the exit of the rocks Littlefoot now called home. It was the yellow door Aaron had walked through just hours ago.

*Odd*, he thought. Littlefoot took note of the confusion that was painted his face with clear strokes.

"What's wrong?" She asked.

"Nothing." He paused and remained locked on the door. "That's the door that brought me here. Never seen them move before."

Littlefoot was quick to answer. "Did it move because I did?"

She had a point. Littlefoot's world had now changed. Her home was different, maybe the entrance to it was different now, too.

Aaron simpered. "Maybe it did."

His stare stayed fixed on the door. He wasn't sure that was time to leave yet. At one point he'd have paid to have it appear, but now, he wasn't so adamant.

Littlefoot kicked her feet in rhythm against the floor. She stood up and turned the television on. A military drumroll struck Aaron's ears from the very first snare-hit, and as he looked, he saw the show. *The Sisters Three*. He grinned. A facial motion that was stacked to the very edges with fond memory.

"It's okay, you can go," said Littlefoot. She meant it. He could hear it.

Aaron smiled and hugged her one last time as she sat by him. "You gonna be okay now?"

"I think I will," she replied.

Aaron stood from the bed and aimed for the door. Happy with the resolution, he was ready for anything that came his way next, whatever that may be.

"Wait!" Shouted Littlefoot as he neared his exit. She ran up behind him and the soles of her shoes clacked against the rock floor.

"You forgot this!"

She handed him the black mask that had fallen from his pocket as he got up.

Aaron patted his pocket down just to be sure. It wasn't there.

"Thank you," he said as he grabbed it. He wondered how that mask wasn't long gone by now. Persistent little thing. He stuffed it back in its home a bit firmer. It wasn't going to fall out again.

"And this," said Littlefoot. She pulled up on the bottom of the dirty white, baggy jumper she wore.

"You keep that one," Aaron insisted. It stopped her in her tracks.

"You sure? What if you get cold?"

He scrunched his face playfully. "What if you do? Keep it. A gift from me."

Littlefoot didn't know how to react. She'd never been given anything before. She stroked her palm on Aaron's shoulder and awkwardly ran back to her bed. She looked happy as she continued to watch her show, with her arm around her bears.

A sliver of peace rested within Aaron as he turned and opened the door.

One last look to Littlefoot as she sat there, unafraid... and free. They shared a wave that said, 'see you soon,' as he walked through, and with a pulse of white light, he and the door were gone.

The island room that filled with doors had become ever-more frustrating for Aaron. Like a steep driveway in icy winters, unpredictable would be the next steps he took, regardless of how careful he took them.

He looked around for a clock but wasn't surprised when there was none. Nothing gave him even the slightest clue, he was just lost in a void of time with no telling. Anything would have been helpful, but to avoid the temptation of another break from the unknown, up and down the row of doors he paced. A few turns of the same old doorknobs and the next one that responded was a plain white one.

*Normal door... suits me,* he thought. In his head, if it wasn't a fancy door, it wasn't a door that would test him. As was the cycle by now, he opened it, took a breath, and pushed through.

As the door closed behind him, a smiley face appeared central on the side he'd opened. Painted with blood, the brush strokes were as clear as the blood itself. It dropped down to the floor until small puddles began to form. It was like the door itself, was bleeding. Then a bow appeared from nothing as if it was born of the air. It too, tainted with blood.

It was the door he was warned about. The door with the bow. Aaron had just entered Stephanie's world, and he didn't even know it.

# 10

## STEPHANIE'S WORLD

Pitch black. Not a millimetre in front of his face could Aaron see. The ground beneath him was firm, though. That was as good a start as any.

A small, faint line of light crept in from what looked like a doorway ahead of him. The closer he got, the more he could see. Funny how eyesight would work like that. The light stole a pathway through the small gap at the bottom of the door, but it proved not enough, and the light that did break through, wouldn't have even been competition for the smallest of candles.

*Oh, thank God*, Aaron thought. His hand finally grabbed the handle after some aimless floundering.

Daylight rushed through the storage cupboard he stood in as he opened the door, it practically blinded him. Through the small gaps between his fingers, as he opened his guarded eyes, Aaron's usual disorientation and loss for words were replaced with a sudden sense of normality.

He was standing in a bakery. A bare, yet functional bakery, specifically one for cakes, he noticed as he glanced around. It smelled of flour and sugar, and the stretched glass display on his left showcased an abundance of muffins and frosted cupcakes.

Truthfully, it only elevated the hunger that already wrestled with Aaron's stomach, to new levels.

There wasn't much else interesting. Just some two-seat tables tucked to the right, in a neat presentation on the black and white checkerboard floor. A handful of displays in the boastful windows that fronted the shop, its framed painted in a lovely mint-green. It was… ordinary, all things considered.

"I can deal with this," Aaron muttered. "No offence, Littlefoot, but being an inch tall… was a little too much—"

A commotion began to arise outside the dainty building he was standing in, in the small, isolated street it was a part of. Just past the large, single-pane glass windows that stood even taller than he, Aaron's eyes filled with the sharp, bright colours that met them.

Like something from a child's show, everything was exaggerated by the colours of the rainbow. From the lines of small businesses that lined the street, to the teams of civilians that wore masks on their faces, yet the most psychedelic attire.

An odd-looking gentleman who wore a brown pin-stripe suit walked past the window. "Hello there!" He said, in a heavily British and well-spoken voice.

It was hard to tell if he was talking to Aaron or not, given the mask that covered his face; an all too familiar device by then.

Aaron had never seen such an exaggerated… flamboyant walk before. It was almost like the man was – acting it?

As he lacked the want to muster any unwanted attention in what had shaped up to be another weird world, Aaron simply greeted the man with the gesture of tipping his hat. He figured it would work, the man seemed friendly enough, so he tried it.

A quick-cut stop flashed his hand down when he realised the fellow hadn't even greeted him, but another masked resident in the street. Aaron's cheeks began to burn as he focused elsewhere with haste.

The street was full of indecipherable chatter. Whistles and shouts. A conglomerate of noise swept through the cake shop like a sly breeze that tickled its way through Aaron's ears. He did half wonder what it was all about. Then, as he stood frigid behind the window, Aaron could just about see the woman as she arrived, much to the delight of the onlookers.

She wore the brightest red ball dress he'd ever seen. Whoever it was, she pushed through the crowd as it parted like the red sea to Moses. Closer, something sat neatly perched on the bun of her blonde hair. What was it? Maybe a crown? Aaron, no doubt, would have bet 'ten' that this finely dressed woman wore Rhian's face. There was no way it wasn't her.

A presentation like that deserved a closer look. Aaron wasn't just there to watch, after all. But as he leaned himself closer to the window like a nosey neighbour, his hand pushed firm on the Perspex tier display that sat below him. Crash!

It threw Aaron down as it kicked his hand out in its collapse, and he slammed against the floor with a dead weight. It looked like he'd been tackled by an invisible forward in a high-octane rugby match. It sent an ache that travelled from his knees right up to his ribs.

"Shit!" He grumbled.

He grabbed a fine-looking box of cakes that had fallen with him, intent on fixing his mess. But his clumsiness caught the attention of a civilian outside.

Aaron defaulted to cowardice and panic. He shot for the abyssal cupboard he'd not long struggled to exit, just as the brown-suited man began to approach.

Of course, he first and foremost looked in desperation for the door that led him back to the island, but there was none. Why would there be? That was an unwelcome pattern. He was stuck there. A box of muffins and no hope.

"Think Aaron, think!"

The door chimed the cast iron bell as it opened and collided with it, and the stranger entered with his right foot first.

With one hand that struggled to balance the dinged cardboard box of treats, Aaron patted his body down with the other, in a frantic search for a miracle.

A shot in the dark, he pulled the black mask from his back pocket. He pulled it over his face with just one hand. It was awkward, to say the least, but he made it work.

The footsteps grew louder outside the door. Aaron took a hefty gulp that kicked at his throat, cracked his neck with a controlled side-to-side slant and opened the door.

"Cake, anyone?" Aaron chirped, as he opened the lid of the box with a brisk lift.

"Ha!" Laughed the well-spoken man. Up close, his brown suit was actually a marvel to see. Dashing, almost. "You sly fox, you!"

He grabbed a blue-iced cake from the box, lifted the chin of his mask, and took a hungry bite.

"Good, right?" Aaron placed the box on the small table to his right. He grabbed a cake for himself and mimicked the chin-lift on his own mask as he slung the baked treat down his gullet.

His mouth still full after his large bite, the man agreed. "64 by the way, and you, sir?"

What on earth did that sentence even mean?

"Sorry?" Aaron choked through a display of projectile crumbs.

"Your name, dear boy. What is your name?"

"Oh, Aaron. You are?"

The suited man chuckled in a deep, raspy tone. "64." His eyes locked to Aaron's. "Can you understand me?"

Aaron put the last half of his cake on the box beside him. He brushed his hands against the thigh of his trousers.

"Sorry, your name is a… number?"

It was odd that this… stranger would question the legitimacy of his name.

"My *name* is 64."

Aaron sighed. "Your *name*… is 64?"

64 tutted. Loud. It echoed through the room almost as much as his firm-bottomed snakeskin loafers. "And yours is Aaron."

"Y-Yeah… It's an ordinary name."

157

"Are you suggesting mine isn't, boy? How long have you been here?" He mocked. "Five minutes?" The sarcasm dripped from his crumby guffaw like a leaky faucet as it shot out pieces of cake, like mortar fire.

Aaron shifted his head back until his chin was in line with his chest. He looked left, he looked right. Then his eyes fixed on the man's shoes.

"Maybe a little bit longer, but yeah, pretty much. I came through—"

64 threw the remainder of his cake, little as it was, on the floor. He grabbed the slack of Aaron's jumper sleeve and dragged him into the cupboard.

Aaron only wished he'd known the light switch in the cupboard was right next to the door as 64 flicked it; it would have helped him just minutes before. Also glad, that he didn't slip down the staircase that sat three feet left of where he walked through the first door in complete darkness, as 64 led him down them, into the basement and thrashed him with an onslaught of questions he wasn't ready for.

Below, between the unkept array of boxes and baking supplies that sat on flimsy wooden shelving that bowed beneath the weight, and the lines and lines of cookery books piled across the floor, Aaron and 64 stood face-to-face with each other at opposite ends of a near-collapsed wooden table.

The light that dangled in a sway offered an inconsistent sunset glow. It was hard to make out 64, given he was masked. Aaron pinched his eyes into focus.

"What do you want?" He asked, to the small fraction of the man he could see.

"So," the darkness replied. "Your arrival has changed things." 64 stood a bit closer. Aaron could see him better now.

"How?" Aaron pulled off his mask, his hair had seen better days. Even right after waking his hair would be less... disfigured. The man opposite him seemed taken aback by it all.

As 64 wiped the food that clung to his chin, with his bare hand, he asked, "You can do what no other can, here, she's oblivious to it, is she not?"

Then his articulate delivery switched in an instant as he clenched his hands together in desperation.

"You can free us, ain't it," he said, in a more common dialect. Aaron took a step back and just stared at him. It felt like a whole other person had stepped into the room.

"Listen," said 64, still in a cockney interpretation. "All you gotta do is bump 'er off. Simple yeah?"

Aaron shook his head. *This can't be real*, he thought. *This place is messing with me.* He placed his hands on the table and leant in, closer.

"Bump her off? Like, kill? I don't even know who *she* is. In fact, I don't even know who you are. All you're doing here is freaking me out, and considering what I've seen today, that's a damn hard job to do."

The well-spoken 64 replaced the cockney like someone flipped a switch and he changed channels.

"I do apologise. He just… finds a way to slip out sometimes." He straightened his suit.

"The little pillock," he muttered.

Aaron needed a moment. His head felt not unlike a beaten and bruised apple.

"Are… Are you alright?" He asked.

"Absolutely," replied 64. Then he sighed. "You get used to it."

Aaron stood tall again and folded his arms. "Let's start with who *she* is, shall we?"

It took 64 a good while to find the stones to explain everything. Long enough that Aaron could swipe the crumbs from his t-shirt. Long enough that his mind could drift off and remember why he was there. Soon, he became impatient.

"Oi." Aaron snapped his fingers. The British man recoiled back from his thoughts.

"Right you are. She… she likes to be called Stephanie—"

"Stephanie? Shit." The name alone forced Aaron into a genuine panic.

"You know her?"

Aaron sucked the air between his teeth, then stuck his tongue into his cheek. He looked to the dull light.

"No, but I've heard the name."

"When?"

"When I was warned to avoid this place." Aaron's hand caressed his forehead. "There was no bow on the door. I was told to avoid *the door with the bow*."

64 laughed under his breath. "If Stephanie doesn't want you to see the bow… you won't see it, my boy."

Another puzzle Aaron had to figure out on his own, but more important matters were at bay. First, and most importantly, why 64 wanted her gone.

"Ah," he said. He looked to the table in a sulk. "We're not free, you see." He was ramped, ready to reel off a full speech, but he noticed the sound of Aaron's heel as it tapped away on the dust layered floor.

Quick to get to the point, he rounded his information up. He and the many civilians of the town were bound to Stephanie's will. That any of them, no matter who, chose free will over her rulership, always disappeared never to be seen again. There was no discrimination in who was next.

"Please, help us. If you want to leave… I'm sorry but that is what it will take. I can see your eyes wander in hope of an exit."

Aaron flicked his wandering eyes back to the man. "I can't kill anyone, 64. That's not the answer."

"Wrong, my boy. It's the *only* answer. Take that as an informed evaluation from a man who just wants to be free. To live. If you find yourself not believing me—" 64's demeanour shifted again.

"Then go look for ya 'self ain't it. Don't be a mug an' just sit 'ere believin' me." Then he switched back. He growled with a breath.

"You know, he's right. See it with your own eyes first. You'll come around, boy." It seemed 64 had little control of his changes. But that was because he didn't. Thankfully, for him, that was something Aaron *had* grown accustomed to.

Composed, Aaron wanted just one thing from 64 before he offered any help.

"Take off your mask," he demanded. The look that he received was less than convincing. "If you want trust, I need to see *you*. Not the first time I've sung this tune, 64."

"T—sir, you must be pulling—"

Aaron's wide eyes fixed on the suited man. The stare he shot across the table was more than enough to back 64 into a corner.

"Right you are." 64 slowly peeled his mask up, until it flopped in his hand above his head, and Aaron's own face stared back at him.

It was like a mirror. The same lines of dirt that smeared his cheekbone, the same flakes of soil in his eyebrows, and the same messed hair. It was plain as day, even in the gloom of the basement. 64 was somehow an exact reflection of he who forced him to remove his mask.

A more demented stare forced 64 to re-fit his mask. He waited for Aaron to come around, and at least hoped it wouldn't take as long as he feared it would. It was the reason he'd hesitated to remove his cover. That can't have been easy on Aaron.

# 11

## STEPHANIE

Returning that which once forced him back to reality, 64 snapped his fingers until Aaron responded.

"I did try and warn—"

Aaron clenched his lips. "Not gonna question it," he said. "There's literally no point." Aaron felt like despite what world he walked into, the next would always one-up the previous. Really, he should have seen that twist coming.

"I wouldn't have an answer to share, anyway, I'm afraid," said 64.

Aaron was curious what 64's plans were for him. He also, through no fault of his own, couldn't shake the necessity to help. That seemed to be what he was there for.

"Lay it on me then."

He was met with a quizzical look, one that never left him. He reiterated, "Tell me how I end this."

The two men discussed a plan of action as the time ticked by around them. 64 was awfully shady about it and spent most of his time whispering into Aaron's ear. How long it had been, it was hard to tell in the pitiful swamp of illumination they called a basement. The street above them had quietened. No commotion or movement. The first ounce of pure silence since Aaron had arrived. He could the faint creaks within the room as its questionable walls swayed just a fraction.

64 passed a sharp cake-knife to Aaron, that he'd scavenged from the depths of the clutter around him. Its handle was dressed in white plastic that proudly wore a floral design. The blade was wrapped in parchment paper. He had a reel of duct tape in his other hand.

"And this is the only way?" Aaron lifted his shirt and held the knife lengthways across his chest as 64 began to fix it on with the tape.

"The only way to keep us all safe," the man said. His eyes dropped a level. "To set us free."

Aaron stole a look at 64 whilst he pressed the tape flush. It clung to his skin like a rash.

"Ready to make some noise, sir?" Asked 64.

"I guess." He figured if he played along, he'd be able to leave. A bluff, to be exact.

Later, while the pavements were empty and the sun had set, the street Aaron had once peered upon looked like a ghost town. It rested within the grey tones of the night, not a streetlamp in sight. If anything, at the time it was peaceful and lovely.

Banners and confetti blew with the light wind in a loose dance and tickled the street as they danced across it. The only thing that sat in more loneliness than the world around him was the sanity that Aaron, himself, once held.

He burst through the door of the bakery as loud as he could and stood in the middle of the street. A single look down at the mask that lay dormant in his clenched fist, and he stuffed it deep in the pocket it now called home.

With a crash so loud it could deafen, the dented metal bin Aaron threw decimated the window of Smiler's Fruit Shop opposite him and ripped down its lovely basket display. A wince crossed his face as he did it. A look of displeasure and regret, but it had to be shaken off.

He ran up and down the length of the street and banged away at the doors. In his rampage, he kicked over every bin and mailbox before him.

"Look at this guy!" He bellowed in tone-deaf song. "No mask don't care. Freedom for everybody! Come say hello!"

In his own little world, something about the disturbance he had created began to ease him. Stress relief, maybe. Aaron could see why some of Rhian's angry alternates resorted to violence; it was quick and effective. But maybe he took it a little too far, as he trashed the place with a racket so loud it could've woken the deaf.

His brief, yet potent delve into criminal damage came to a close when he was struck from behind. A swift slam from the tip of a metal baseball bat and it was lights out for he who had disturbed the peace.

"Ugh." The lump on the back of his head resembled the shape and texture of a golf ball. It stuck out a good inch and a half and pulsed a pain through him in sync with his heartbeat.

He'd have had it covered with the palm of his hand if he could, but they were both strapped to the back of the metal chair he was slumped on. Some rusted chicken wire wrapped lousily around them that balanced the line between securing and cutting off his wrists.

The bright spotlight that flicked on inside the concealed room stuck out more than a little bit. It highlighted Aaron and the chair inside an arena of white luminescence like he was the star of the show.

"Hello," groaned Aaron. The light forced his eyes shut. It was a struggle to try and open them.

"Heyyyy," sang an angelic voice from nowhere.

Shadow first, Stephanie twirled her way into the circle of light. Her red silk dress gleamed and reflected it all right back to Aaron. Now she was the star, centre stage, and she stole the show.

The pale contrast of her skin highlighted the smears of blood that splashed upon her cheeks like a Jackson Pollock canvas. She twisted down to Aaron's level until her thick-lined eyes met the level of his. He refused the eye contact and turned down to look upon her bloodied white heels. It didn't matter where he looked, she was covered in blood. She may as well have been sponsored by the stuff.

Stephanie was the psychotic and unstable one. The very reason Ember shot her warning. This evaluation… Stephanie made *very* clear to Aaron.

"Where's ya come from then?" The knife she'd ripped from Aaron's chest pressed at the point to his chin.

She laughed in hysterics. The only thing that moved as she did was her jaw like she was some kind of faulty animatronic. She wiped a tear from her eye as it smudged the black make-up that lined it. "Break the rules much?" she barked.

Aaron groaned. His head felt like it had been caught between the collision of two planets. "Jesus," he moaned. "Stephanie then?"

He took a single look above the bun that sat on her head and smirked. "Barbed wire, of course." The crown she sported was also bloodied. Because why wouldn't it be. His thoughts at the bakery were right, the woman in red was the next part of Rhian.

"Stylish," he remarked.

Stephanie lowered the knife. She kissed Aaron's forehead. It left a rose-red imprint he'd have loved to wipe right off.

"Hey there, new guy!" She exclaimed. An unmistakable excitement that served to freak Aaron even more. Her mood had switched in an instant, faster than a fired bullet.

"Yeah, hi. So, what made you then?" Aaron tried to sit less arched in the chair, but his restraints prevented it as they pulled him down. His words collided with every grunt and moan that leaked from him.

"Life," she said, in love.

Aaron scrunched his face as the embodiment of crazy flung her arms high into the air and spun into a pirouette. Then with no hesitation, she geared the knife to his chin again and lowered her tone into a growl.

"Answer my question!"

Even the air around Aaron began to question what exactly was on display. Not one single sentence had the same delivery from Stephanie, no single emotion was consistent. Stephanie had reeled off on an unpredictable, switcheroo that played with him.

*Karma*, he thought. Just a single word that made sense to him. He shrugged off 64's reveal thinking it couldn't get any madder, then there he was, chair – knife – Stephanie.

Aaron didn't know if he could die in Stephanie's world, but if 64 held any level of honesty, he wasn't about to take any chances. He'd not feared one of Rhian's counterparts as much as Stephanie. This one was different, the capriciousness of her kept him on edge. With whatever water his words could hold, it was time he tried to simmer the fire.

"Hey, I'm new here," he said. He acted like there wasn't a knife pointed at him. "How am I supposed to know what the rules are?"

Stephanie mocked him in a babble, just like a toddler would. "Blah blah blah…" The hand that didn't threaten Aaron with a knife, folded open and shut with her words. A pale, bony puppet.

"Nope," she tutted. "Supposed to cover ya damn face!"

The point of the knife pushed beneath Aaron's skin by a fraction as she pushed his head back with it. With a whisp of her finger, Stephanie wiped the blood that spawned from the cut she'd made.

"Sorry sweetie," she whispered. Then she kissed it better. Another lip print for him to wipe away later.

"Look, I don't know you. I haven't been here long. So… tell me about yourself, I'm all ears." And he was, too. He was… interested.

"Pffffft!" She spat a little.

"No, seriously, Stephanie. If we're ever to get along, we have to start somewhere, right?"

She took a second. "Okay!"

A wide smile crossed her face and all of a sudden, she looked like the happiest person ever. Her demeanour could have rivalled Dolly's. Then it turned to a snarl as she scrunched her face. A rasp in her voice as she growled her next words.

"Mummy didn't play nice!"

Then the smile came back, filled with wonder and butterflies. "It's okay though, it happens, don't it?"

Stephanie gasped. "Have you seen the pretty colours outside, they're so pretty!"

Her face turned back to within an inch of Aaron's, and she glared into his soul. "You… broke… my… shops!"

"Yikes." Aaron's jaw was stiff, his head locked back at the most awkward angle as he tried to escape Stephanie's stare of a thousand deaths. The wire around his wrists began to dig like they were hungry.

"Sorry I asked."

Stephanie's voice began to break as her eyes reddened. "W-why ya sorry, darlin'?"

Aaron shook his head. "Mmm, nope." He didn't want to answer that. The last thing he wanted was to tell her what was in *his* head at that moment.

He wasn't really given much choice, though. Through stares and pleas, bounces between anger and sadness, she drew out his answer as if it were attached to a rope she'd pulled.

"You're a fuckin' basket case." It slipped from him like a tick. "I'm sorry. I didn't wanna say that out loud but they're the only words I have right now. Whatever that was…" He looked her up and down. "Nope."

The erratic woman just laughed it away as she wielded the knife just inches from Aaron's face. If Aaron thought mere words could hurt Stephanie, clearly, he didn't know her very well. She edged to him, without a single blink until the point of the knife sat with intent between his eyes.

"Ya know, you sound just like the rest of 'em. Always me, me, me, but never listenin'. Bad as 'em all, you are." She turned and walked away as she said something in the drone of mumble.

"Ask me what made me then shut me out like some kinda…" she muttered. Aaron couldn't hear it all, but he knew he needed an out. He couldn't appeal to her wants, exactly; he wasn't sure if she had any. Though, his conversation with 64 gave him a 'bright' idea.

"Oi," he yelled. Stephanie snatched her head back.

She said nothing, but her eyes spoke plenty as they narrowed with the angle of her brows. Aaron decided to play her game. He slouched the inch his restraints would let him and kicked the world. Why not join her for a careless moment?

"Why don't you just… kill 'em all?"

"What ya saying?" Stephanie snapped.

"Ahh, you know, those little shits that think they can run around and do what they want. To hell with Stephanie's rules and all that nonsense they talk behind your back. Just kill 'em. Job done." Aaron shrugged his shoulders… he couldn't wipe his hands together.

Stephanie smiled. She bit her bottom lip.

"Ohh, I like you." She walked closer to the man who'd finally spoken her language. "Tell me more," she pleaded.

"Oh, I don't think I can say the next part out loud," said Aaron. Mischief riddled his eyes and Stephanie was hooked. Just as expected. Mischief was a drug to her.

She leant down to his ear and giggled. "Tell me." She was so anxious to hear it. But Aaron wanted to tease her a while longer. He'd dance around it until she couldn't contain her want any longer.

As the shake of her giggle wrapped around her words, she said, "I want to know."

Aaron leaned his lips as close as he could to her ear and slowly opened them with his whisper. "No, no. I want to see the look in your eyes when I tell you".

Stephanie giggled again, hot and flustered. She repositioned her head before his. Their eyes locked and Aaron smiled. It made Stephanie smile too. The devilish intent was almost fully cooked, but not in the way she had hoped.

Aaron had structured the entire false encounter as a diversion while he loosened the sharp wire that imprisoned his wrists. He found enough slack to free them and threw his head back sharp. As he cleared his face of the knife in her hand, Aaron kicked his legs to the side of hers as hard as he could. She fell to the ground in a daze and hit her shoulder pretty hard. He didn't want to do that, but she hardly gave him a choice whilst he sat in fret for his life.

Aaron shot himself out of the chair. He took a moment to massage his wrists, then the back of his head... then the cut on his chin. Most of his body was hurt in some sense of the word by now.

Stephanie kicked and screamed in hysterics. She snapped back and forth between threats and begs.

"Please, don't kill me." Then she kicked her legs out into his shins. "I'll kill *you*."

Aaron picked her up and gently put her on the chair. He gave her wrists the same treatment she gave his.

"Why would you do this?" she sobbed.

She spat at him. "Do you know who I am? I'll—"

"Yeah, yeah. You'll *kill* me," Aaron mocked. His hand opened and closed like a puppet. "Blah blah blah."

Finally, he could take a breath, so he closed his eyes, hands on his hips, and just relaxed for a moment. Now he could talk with reason.

"So, when you said, 'mummy didn't play nice,' you meant she hurt you, right?"

Stephanie said nothing through her scoff. She growled, almost barked as she threw her head forward. Aaron didn't know whether to feel bad for her or be glad she was tied up. The knife she'd dropped lay near his feet and gave him a pretty good answer.

He took a very deep, long-winded breath, through which, his inner 'doctor' came out.

"I don't think you know." He kicked the knife away. "I think whatever she did… you didn't know whether to laugh it off, cry about it, pretend everything was okay… or be angry." His eyes looked to the light. Then he nodded. "I'm sorry I hurt you."

He picked his head up and locked eyes with Stephanie. She saw the sorrow that looked at her.

"I really am. I just… reacted to it all. The knife in your hand, the pulsing of my head – I just didn't know what you would do. I'm sorry."

Stephanie leant her head forward, as far as she could. Her eyes showed pity until they narrowed, and she hurled a heaped cannon of spit that slapped against Aaron's cheek.

"No, you ain't," she hissed. "Time's up, anyway, do what ya wanna."

Aaron struggled. His eyes stayed fixed on the floor as the spit dripped off his cheek and down onto it. He closed them. Just to get a moment of peace. It seemed to be the only thing that worked for him. But… what did she mean, 'time's up?'

He'd been in his solace for two ticks of the big hand when from nowhere, came a cheer that rip-roared through his ears and shot his heart half a mile from his chest.

He was stood, high on a platform that rose three feet from the ground. On a stage that overlooked every resident of Stephanie's town. Forty, maybe fifty masked applauders. Whistles and cheers rose above it all. It threw him completely off balance, both literally and figuratively.

The feedback of the microphone squealed to his left as 64 clasped it and ran toward him. The loafers made a right noise on the planks of the stage while they approached Aaron, still dizzy from the flash-change of scenery.

"You did it, sir! You captured her!" He shouted. The microphone was so loud it almost deafened even the onlookers.

Aaron smiled, nervous. "This wasn't the plan."

64 hushed him. He was so proud, his eyes glinted like fresh-polished glass. He pulled a gun from his waistline; a beautiful, white-handled revolver with a black floral pattern painted on it with care. He passed it to Aaron and the crowd began to chant.

"Kill her… Kill her!" They droned, between the sound of their united claps.

"A gun?" Aaron looked at it in disgust. "What about the knife?"

64 chuckled. "Do you *see* the knife?" He shrugged sharply. "Or do you see the firearm?"

He turned to the crowd and yelled into his microphone. "Empty the chamber and free us, saviour!"

The crowd got even louder. Aaron could feel the vibrations of their chants through the elevation of the stage. Maybe now he was just a hair away from earning his exit.

Aaron held the barrel against the back of Stephanie's head while she laughed through her restraints. He crept his finger to the trigger with a single slide. He waited.

"Do it, pussy," Stephanie challenged. She laughed some more and then changed again. A beg. "Please don't."

One millimetre. The trigger creaked. It took a stronger pull than he thought. He took the same millimetre in reverse when his finger let go.

"No."

He threw his armed hand into the sky and fired off all six rounds. It startled 64 and the crowd before him. Even Stephanie took to a flinch. Then he threw the gun to the suited man's feet as it smoked from the barrel.

"I won't," he said.

64 pinched his fingers almost fully together "But sir, we're this close-"

"Hey!" firmed Aaron. No microphone was needed, his shout was loud enough that the crowd grew silent. Even the wind calmed. 64 locked his jaw tight and slipped a gulp.

"I won't do it. I know… right, I _know_ if I do, you all get freedom, okay, I do. But I can't – won't. That woman…" He shot his finger to Stephanie.

"She's part of someone much bigger. She's part of a family I don't intend on breaking – messed up as they are, it's a mess that… well there's no-one else's mess I'd rather be part of.

"Yeah, she knocked me down, and maybe she's a few apples short of a basket but…"

Aaron turned to the hushed crowd. Their murmurs stopped as they all faced him. Aaron raised his voice above them all. It carried well through the street.

"All of you just think. For one small second just ask yourself why she's the way she is. She needs help, not punishment. The more you shun someone who's already been rejected, the worse you make them."

He looked back to 64, who, whilst warm, began to shiver.

"You want her dead?" He shoved him back a few steps with a sharp throw of his arms. "Kill her yourself. I won't. Even if it means my chances of getting out of here are gone."

"B-but, y-you'll… you'll n-never leave," stammered 64.

"So be it." Aaron was done. Exhausted. He was on the verge of giving up. He went from being stood in a bakery, to standing on a stage where he'd pointed a gun at someone who wore Rhian's face, in what felt like a single gust of wind. His hopes had been drained, and he caved to his own heart as it stole his only exit from beneath his feet.

He strolled over to where Stephanie was seated, loosened the wire that claimed her wrists and helped her to her feet with a hand under her arm. He forced a double-take to 64, and a stare that lingered over the crowd before he gestured 64 to give him the microphone, which he did, fast.

Aaron lifted the device to his lips.

"You know what? Seeing as I'll be sticking around longer than planned. If I hear anything… *anything* has happened to Stephanie, it won't be her you'll need to worry about, got it?"

Only silence responded to him, but that was enough. Silence, after all, spoke on its own.

He turned his mouth to Stephanie's ears.

"I'm sorry," he said.

Through Stephanie's laugh, she asked, "What ya sorry for this time, cry-baby?"

Aaron looked around the entire town. The buildings, the people, the sky. He had one last whisper to share with her.

"That you were robbed of more than this. You deserved better."

Aaron strolled off the stage in a huff and knocked into 64's shoulder as he slung the microphone at his feet. He made for his target; the cupboard that started it all, and he stayed there for what he thought would be forever. No plans and no hopes, just a sulk. Like any normal human being.

He'd sat for a handful of lonely moments in the gloom of the storage cupboard. Even though he knew where the light switch was, he chose to slum it in darkness. He blocked out the world, figured maybe he'd made a mistake. Killing Stephanie would have opened that door and he'd be one step closer. But he wasn't a killer. Not in general, not even if someone deserved it, and especially when his target wore Rhian's face. He'd accepted his fate.

Then, within his mope, light flooded the miserable room. Though, not a light by definition... more the glow from a door he accepted he'd never see again.

*It can't be*, he thought. But he wasn't going to wait around and find out. Aaron pounced for the door, snatched at the handle, and let the white abyss swallow him as he got the hell out of there in a rush.

Back in the town, Stephanie rubbed her wrists as she stood next to 64. The crowd behind them walked off into the distance, back to their lives, and whatever it was they'd usually be doing.

"That... was different," 64 said.

Stephanie just smiled as she looked back at the chair. A warmth overwhelmed her from inside. "Yeah, it was, weren't it? Could've sworn he'd do it..."

"Looks like we were wrong for once."

Stephanie looked at 64. A laugh slipped, but she caught most of it. It sounded like… happiness.

"Played our game pretty well, huh?"

64 asked, "Do you think he'll return?" Then he began to fade until he was barely visible. His form, whatever was left of it, merged with Stephanie like a soul returning home.

"I hope so," Stephanie whispered as she walked away. "I like that one."

Stephanie had put Aaron through his paces in the time he spent on her street, and he was oblivious to it all. To him, it was another and a mission failed, but he couldn't have been more wrong.

On the island, to wait around was to be a fool as Aaron thought he'd made the greatest and luckiest escape of all time. Only one door remained in what was once a stretch of six: the black one.

At that point, only one personality, that he knew of, was left. Whisper. He hadn't met her in his travels yet, but he was most familiar with her appearances *up top*, where she'd sit in hunkered silence from the moment of her arrival, right until her departure. In eighteen months, Aaron had seen Whisper the most. She was the most frequent, and the most recent, on the night before Rhian's incident.

With a slight twist of the knob and a few steps forward, he'd stepped into her threshold. Or at least, that's what he thought.

# 12

## HALLWAY VOICES

A cloud of grey and red would swirl. An endless hallway void of any light or life. Hisses and hushed, distorted voices all met Aaron as the door slammed shut behind him, and zapped away in a flash of red light, similar to how an old tv would switch off. Scarce yet controlled, he steadily moved forward, deeper into the unknown.

His heel stumbled as it touched ground earlier than he expected. Courtesy of not an ounce of light. Above, a whining hiss got louder and louder, as did screeches and howls until something pushed Aaron hard into a wall he never saw coming. It happened again… then again. Until he was forced to remain against the wall.

"Stop!" He yelled. He couldn't see what he'd hurled his demand at; he aimed it into thin air.

He soon wished he hadn't, as the whirling mass above him began to riddle with a sequence of beady red glows. Eyes opened… tens of pairs of them. Through a crowded gather much like a murmuration, they hovered in a dance just feet above Aaron's head.

And then… the voices came.

"Aaron," whispered an echoed undertone that repeated itself into oblivion. Like it was spoken into an empty concert hall. It stood the hairs on his arms.

"So scared," it taunted.

It continued to rally its remarks. Aaron began to shrivel up as he felt his back dead against the wall masked in darkness. Goosebumps invaded every inch of his skin until it felt like sandpaper, and the taste of pennies overrode his senses.

"You can't save her," it said. "Too weak." Like beating a dusty rug, the demented voices lashed away at Aaron's soul with no remorse. He would have covered his ears if it made even the slightest difference.

They wouldn't stop, the voices, until Aaron was crushed with his own body weight against the solid resistance he was thrown against, crouched, knees bent up against his chest. He begged them to stop, for one moment of sanity. But they were too loud.

"Go away." He looked into the abyss of red, grey, and black. "Stop."

But *it* had other ideas.

"Weak…" The words lingered as long as three whole breaths. More voices, all spoke at the same time in another droned jab. "Trapped."

"Stop!" Aaron's plea slipped through frozen lips and off a tongue that quivered.

The voices invaded his mind like a nightmare and played on repeat until all that was left was for Aaron's will to break.

The unknown laughed back. A sadistic, wheeze of a chuckle with bass so profound it vibrated Aaron's ears inside and out. The relentless prods continued. Like… torture. They enjoyed it like it was a game.

"You… will… never… find…" The silence. For almost five whole seconds before the voice barked Rhian's name so loud that Aaron's body tried to leap through the solid wall he cowered against.

His soul shattered and his mind collapsed, whilst his heart skipped more than a couple of beats. Then a flash of red light shot through the hallway, and it swallowed everything in sight.

A cloud of grey and red would swirl. An endless hallway void of any light or life. Hisses and hushed, distorted voices all met Aaron as the door slammed shut behind him, and zapped away in a flash of red light, similar to how an old tv would switch off. Scarce yet controlled, he steadily moved forward, deeper into the unknown.

He'd been here before, the exact same moment. He didn't know what was worse, the hallway, or the second dose of Groundhog Day. His heartbeat raced, and he planted his steps in mute. In slow motion. But it wasn't enough. It was never going to be.

"Aaaarrrroooonnnn." Like it fed on the fear it provoked, the voice called to him in eery stretches.

Aaron's sigh pushed out with so much force it almost yanked out his lungs.

"So, this is what you do to them, is it? You enjoy that? Scaring someone into what... submission?"

An ear-shattering hiss knocked the brief confidence from Aaron and jammed his mouth stiff shut. It sounded like someone pierced a bloated tyre.

It knew his fears and it knew his insecurities. It knew his journey so well it repeated it back to him. Out of context, in distorted, echoed voices, they punched their way through Aaron's ears.

"This place, it ain't for you, Haze."

Aaron twisted his head away from the sound. He scrunched his face and he fought.

"That's what *lost* means." A creepy laugh followed it. It was Dolly's, but at the same time, it wasn't.

Aaron tried to resist more.

"Must be out of your mind coming in here…" A devastating screech bounced off every wall and pierced Aaron's brain. "Quite literally."

He slammed to the floor as he held his head. Then it laughed again. Like a demon watching its target with the patience of a predator.

"Everything… is just so… dangerous," it whispered. Every word echoed on itself. Then a high pitch scratch filled everything, like feedback from a microphone.

It pushed Aaron deeper into his buckle. Then, from the abyssal swarm.

"You… broke…my…shops!"

It was so loud it wrestled the thoughts that lay front and centre in Aaron's head. Like a fight to the death, it slammed against the sides of his skull. He couldn't contain his dread… and soon, he found his position, cowered against the same wall once more, with his hands squoze firm against the sides of his head.

"Stop." A pitiful cry for release that was met with more demonic laughter.

"Leeeaaavvvvee." A single word, the length of a common sentence.

Aaron had no intention of that. His crippled soul sat curled into a ball where the wall met the floor and he pushed out one single word.

"No."

A flash of red so bright, it swallowed the room.

A cloud of grey and red would swirl. An endless hallway… another repetition, like that wasn't already a steaming bundle of frustration.

Aaron looked up, dropped his shoulders, and pushed out a lengthy growl. Like an angered hound, his eyes saw a thousand ways to kill the threat that circled him. His body though… weak. Shut down from cycles of terror and fear like it planted a virus in his circuits. An uncontrollable tremor climbed through his legs as he tried to stand tall.

Twenty-three steps. Then the hisses started to bully him once more. A cloud of red eyes opened up, and the voices started.

Aaron couldn't be bothered. He closed his eyes, threw his head back and shook it. For a moment, everything went silent. Not a droplet of sound. He opened his eyes, and it all came back. Closed – gone. Open – there.

Hold on just a minute.

Aaron snatched the black mask from its home in his pocket. He'd never been so happy to see it. He yanked it over his face so fast it practically burned his forehead.

He gave it a trial run. When it covered his eyes, the noises vanished. When he lifted it above them, they came back without fail. Every single time for a rotation of ten.

"Alright then," he said. A grin broke a gap to reveal his teeth as it stretched wide. "Let's play."

With the mask curled at his head, eyes on display, he let out a window-shattering bellow that snatched at the attention of everything in the room. Like a pack of wolves, the masses of chaos caught the scent and raced toward it. Just feet away from him, Aaron slung the mask down over his face one last time and threw his fists to the wind in a flurry.

A lot of them landed, it felt like. As his fists of fury flung in every direction, they hit what mimicked firm pillows. They screeched and hissed with every impact, louder than the shouts Aaron himself, had summoned from deep within. It was like he'd confronted a supernatural storm.

Steam ran low and the punches eventually stopped. Aaron peeked the mask up in the silence and finally, to the content of himself *and* his mind, everything had disappeared. Just a black void of… nothing. Then, a bright flash of the same red he'd seen too many times before. He kept his eyes shut, he couldn't deal with another repetition, he was still tired from the last. But as moments fleeted and nothing made a sound, he opened them. He was glad he chose to.

Dead ahead of him, a new door had appeared where only darkness sat before. A black door, cracked with a crimson glow. From the distance between them, it almost looked like a block of heated coal.

At least it was something. Anything was better than the hallway, so Aaron opened the unusual door. It wasn't hot, even in the slightest, which was odd, given its appearance. No light fed from it as he opened it, which was a first, so his steps were careful as he crossed through, and into what appeared to be, another pit of darkness.

# 13

## WHISPER

Just as many gyrating watchers, cramped in much denser form, filled the tiny box-like room. Though it lacked any cohesive light, the bundle of the eyes that circled above lit it in a faint scarlet burn just enough that Aaron could see the four corners. They couldn't have been much more than four solid strides from touching each other.

The mass of eyes itself took up so much room that Aaron could feel the walls almost close in around him like a compactor.

Growls and screeches, all too familiar, were boxed in with him and suffocated in the same dense air that was packed tight in his lungs.

As Aaron scouted the room for signs of... anything, he could barely make out the small two-seat sofa that sat angled across the left-most corner, right opposite the door. It was uncomfortably close to where he stood. So close, he pondered how he didn't already see it. As he peered behind it, almost as if he knew... he saw her. Whisper. And what a relief it was.

Hair sat upon her shoulders, just like Rhian's, only it was black and frayed. It flickered in the light breeze that swept through the room. A breeze that was caused by the entities that dominated the space above. Her complexion - so pale it almost stood on its own in the dark like a dim, dusty bulb. Her ghostly skin itself was riddled with cracks and breaks like old porcelain. Cracks that would glow with a gentle redness, alive with the same energy that sat in the eyes of the heathens that swam laps above her.

She had but one set of clothes, did Whisper. Black and tatty, ripped at the cuffs and the hems as though she'd lived on the streets for quite some time.

Whisper was clenched, arms clutched around her knees with her fingers interlocked. Huddled into the corner that escaped behind the seats. It was a position that Aaron not only recognised but one he'd been subjected to himself.

Quick to decide, He climbed over the couch and sat with his back against it, opposite the alternate he'd shared the most time outside with.

"Whisper," he said, in restricted decibels.

The tortured woman nodded.

"I'm not here to hurt you," Aaron reassured. He didn't want to move too close; he knew how fragile Whisper was. Instead, he let his words lift her.

She knew, though. She recognised the man who would kiss her forehead. The man who would leave her in silence and not pester her, so her time outside, in contrast to her world, was peaceful – to a degree. She appreciated Aaron and his soft voice.

Aaron pointed his eyes up. "What are they?"

For a moment she retained her silence. Her eyes crept to their corners, and she looked at Aaron. "Demons," she slipped out. The words shook as they left.

"Demons, okay." Aaron bit his bottom lip until it rolled over his lower teeth. His eyes fixed on the demons, as Whisper called them. To him the word alone made sense. He felt them, he heard them. No other word would fit as well. He nodded as he looked back at her.

"They don't leave," she said. "Ever."

She began to rock like a buoy in gentle waves, side to side. The boards that lined the floor under her began to creak with the motion. Aaron, at a gentle pace, reached his arm across until it rested on the hands that wrapped Whisper's legs. She stopped the moment it touched.

"Save me," she cried with no tears. Tears were lost on her already, she'd cried them all away.

Through trials and tribulations, adventure and mischief, and a collective mountain of self-doubt, Aaron finally knew what to say.

"If I save you, how long before it all comes back around? But… maybe I can help you save yourself." He smiled softly. "Just like the others."

Whisper picked her head up fully. It weighed a tonne, and her neck was stiff with rust. "The others?" she asked.

"Sure. Ember, Dolly, Ma'am, Littlefoot—"

"Littlefoot?" Whisper blurted her words out. She didn't mean to. She cleared her throat with the softest cough. Littlefoot was one of the alternates she knew the most. In a way, they both shared similar emotions; fear and vulnerability.

"You met Littlefoot?"

"I did." Aaron leaned in a touch. "Her world was pretty scary too. She figured it out."

Whisper removed the embrace from her knees and straightened her posture. With a few pops and cracks from her fastened back, she sat straight against the wall until her head rested against it. The pain that drowned her bagged eyes forced Aaron's shoulders to sink an inch.

The quiver in her lip came back, and as she fought against it, she stared into the mass of demons.

"They're so loud. When I sleep, they go away, but when I... when I wake..."

She lost her words as her eyes followed the motion of the swirl she stared at.

"They come back again," Aaron added.

Whisper was the most held back. She was constantly unsure of herself. Much like Littlefoot, the fear she held was carried to the surface. It stuck to her like the very skin she wore. Unable to escape it, much like the rest, she'd live in the same torment day in and day out for... well even she didn't know how long. She'd describe it as 'an eternity.'

Like a father would a sick child, Aaron felt a sense of duty with Whisper. He felt protective

Maybe it was that she was so pulled away from her being, or maybe it was the overpowering persistence of the demons that surrounded her, but Whisper lacked any faith in herself. She was convinced she was weak and invisible. No doubt the voices in her room would tell her that, every chance they got.

"You know what you've seen, and dealt with," Aaron said. "For eternity, right?" He returned his hand to Whisper's knee.

"Nothing about that is weak. Just out there…" He pointed his free hand somewhere in the region where he remembered the door was. "I spent what, five minutes in the same misery and torture. Just a few short minutes and it scared me. I didn't like it."

Aaron never told Whisper he'd fought back against the demons. He just told her what she needed to hear, rather than give her false hope.

"I don't like it either," she whimpered. "And now Rhian's gone, hasn't she?"

The words escaped Aaron as he tried to figure out how, or even *how much* she knew, but he didn't have time to find them.

"You wouldn't be here if she wasn't." Whisper read the room with ease, and she picked up on everything.

Part of Aaron felt the weight of the words she spoke. The other part of him was still driven to find a resolution.

"Yeah." He inhaled. "But I'll find her."

"You should ask Rhiannon. She'd know." Whisper removed her gaze from the ceiling and back to him.

Everything faded into a muffle for Aaron as his chin dropped to his chest. Through the dim light, Whisper could see his pupils dance around as they faced the floor.

"Rhiannon – that's her birth name, isn't it?"

Whisper said nothing in response. She figured she'd let Aaron come to his own on that one. As she knew best, to figure it out on your own is to understand it more.

"She protects us from it," she said.

A frown from the man opposite her. "Protects you from what?" Aaron hoped the answer wasn't cryptic.

"The memories."

It only confused him. As far as Aaron knew, each personality held the memories that made them. It was why they were all different. Ember spoke freely of hers. Ma'am was built from memories of a comfort show and Dolly locked hers away to ensure everlasting happiness. Nothing made sense now. Just as he thought he'd figured it out.

"No," said Whisper. "Almost. We remember what *made* us." Her head tilted to the front of the couch. "*She* knows everything."

At the tilt of Whisper's head, a door appeared opposite the sofa. It cast a bright light from underneath that swept the room. Aaron peeked his head slowly, like a shy mole. It was a dull red door. Only something… moved across it. He narrowed his eyes… It was the paint. Alive, like pulsating blood. Okay…

Whisper sure knew a lot about Rhiannon. And Rhian.

"Rhian's probably in the pit."

Aaron turned sharp to face whisper. He could see more of her face now. He smiled. A face he would never tire of.

"The pit?" he asked. He ignored the door, that could wait.

Whisper sniffled. She didn't want to delve into detail, but she'd already said enough to warrant question.

"That's where the monster is." The words alone haunted her more. It stressed her eyes. If only tears would run so she could cry for once.

Aaron's mind went full Sherlock.

*The pit… monster… that's where the monster is… monster… fir—fire monster. Fire monster!*

"Fire monster?" He was convinced his words were isolated in his head, but those last two spurted out.

"What?" Whisper didn't know the specifics. She just knew there was a monster and a pit, and the two were linked, for as long as the island had existed.

They'd sat contemplating the 'monster' for a while. Aaron's mind whiffed of burned oil as it sifted through ideas and scenarios like a machine.

He patted down his t-shirt then placed his hands on the floor. A tender push elevated his head above the couch and the door came back into view.

Whisper knew it deep down; he had no plan to stay, even the voices above her mocked her for it

"Alone," they would say. "Friend leaves."

Her world was anything except open to visitors. But... Aaron turned his head from the door and back to her as she brushed the right side of her hair behind her ear. He slumped back to his seat on the floor with a thud.

"Must leave," droned her bullies. She felt obliged to listen to them.

"Go," said Whisper.

But Aaron remained seated. He thought it would be easy to leave and get one step closer, but something felt amiss about leaving Whisper on her own, right after she'd helped him. Though she'd lived the same through her entire existence, why not try and change things if there was a chance to? Even if it was by the smallest margin. After all, that seemed to be what he did most in his time on the island.

As Whisper flinched at the barks from the demons, Aaron said, "Close your eyes."

Whisper pushed her top lip up with the bottom until it met her nose. Aaron said it again, so she did. She didn't know why, but it had to lead somewhere.

"What do you hear?" Aaron asked.

She took a moment. Waited whilst her ears scanned around her. She heard nothing at all and felt like Aaron had wasted her time.

"Peace," Aaron said. "Now open them."

Again, she followed his words. Only now, the hisses, the voices and the hideous laughs all came back in an instant.

They yelled at her. "Coward hides… we see you." The cower felt necessary again, by reflex.

With a thought so sharp it could shame a scalpel, Aaron pulled out the black mask he'd found more useful than anything thus far. It took a bigger tug to remove than usual considering he was sat on it. It perched limp in his hand as he passed it to Whisper.

"Put this on," he insisted.

She inched her head away. The smell of it forced a scrunched face. Dirt, sweat and smoke. The perfect blend of disgusting.

"Sorry," said Aaron. He smiled with a shrug. "I've used it a few times. That… and whatever it went through on that bear's head."

Whisper looked at the mask, then at Aaron. Another look at the mask.

"The bear was a soldier," he reiterated. "Ma'am's crazy world. Trust me." He winked.

Trust was something Whisper could do when it came to Aaron, even if it wasn't as easy for her as some of the others. She placed the mask over her messy hair and pulled it down slow.

Everything vanished with a single pull.

She was awake, in her room, but nothing was calling her name. Nothing poked at her weakness or laughed in her face. Through the fibres of the mask, she looked up. Nothing was there. No red glow, no clouds that would sling insults.

*How?* she thought.

Emotions that took some adjusting to, were the very ones she felt. Relief. Freedom. Happiness, almost. An incomprehensible weight lifted in the pull of a mask.

Aaron smiled as he watched her head shift angles while she looked around.

"I know it's not much," he said. "But-"

Whisper interrupted. The tension that once strangled her voice was loosened. More clarity reached her throat, she almost sounded like Rhian again.

"It's enough."

It felt like a crime when she pushed her hands against the wall and stood. Never in her existence had she felt so tall. She felt the weight of her body for the first time in her feet. Balance took a moment. The two steps she took felt like she did them wrong, but she felt like she was standing on the peak of the world, looking down.

Aaron stood too. Whisper never realised how tall he was until she sprung her head back to look at him. What she could see of him through what covered her face, she laughed. It was gentle, a slip of emotion she felt she had to mask with her hands.

To Aaron, the swirling mass of demonic hell remained, as did the voices and the noises. To Whisper, for the moment they were gone. They couldn't see her – she couldn't see them. Aaron placed his hands on her shoulders and looked to where he figured her eyes were.

"Only *I* see you now," he said. "There's nothing above you. Just as if you were sleeping, only now… maybe you can carry that peace with you, when you need it."

His chest sunk into his back when Whisper shot in for a hug. Her ear rested snug against his heart and she relished in the embrace. Her breaths matched the only thing she could hear: his heartbeat.

It was returned. Aaron was so proud to see it. It almost made him cry. His hand met the back of her head and rested there.

"Thank you," she Whispered. Her jaw tickled Aaron's chest as she spoke. Then she let him go, and Aaron cupped his hands around her shoulders.

"Remember," he said. "Unopened letters don't mean that nobody wrote to you."

Whisper angled her head.

"Something my Nan used to tell me when things got too much, and I'd block the world out. She also said that not seeing yourself doesn't mean you're invisible to the rest of the world. That, this thing right here…" He pointed to her chest. "As long as this is thumping away, you're loved by somebody."

Whisper didn't know what to say. She understood his words, and they made sense, but at the same time, they felt like lies.

"Do you love me?" she asked.

Aaron's answer left no gap between her words and his. "I love you all. Especially you."

Even though it wasn't seen, Aaron could feel the smile that crossed Whisper's face as it pushed her cheek into his breast.

"Think of it this way," he continued. "You're loved. Even if it's one person, one is enough. Love is love, right? You're strong, you're beautiful. You're… Whisper. Say it for me, who are you?"

"Whisper." It was really quiet, and not what Aaron wanted. She could do better than that.

"Come on, a little louder, pretend I'm the other side of that door. Who are you?"

"Whisper!" It was a bit louder. It was better but quite fitting to her name it was still just a whisper.

Aaron's finger moved to his ear and forced a laugh from her. "I said to be *proud* of it. Wear it because it's yours. What's your name?"

"Whisper" she shouted. The loudest noise she'd ever dared to make. It startled her. Her head lowered with the help of her arms as she shot away from the hug, and she scanned the room. She laughed a single note when nothing snapped back at her. It was like she trod steps through a wild fever dream.

"That's my girl," said Aaron. His smile beamed. "We all wear a mask sometimes. Now you're just one of us."

*One of us*. Those words lifted Whisper's spirits. She was accepted. Is that what acceptance felt like? It made her feel light on her feet.

As she noticed Aaron's quick glance at the door, Whisper said, "Go, but be careful."

"I'm always careful," Aaron joked. Whisper could smell the lies, but she agreed anyway.

"I believe you."

As Aaron took a path to the door, he had one last thing to say, because he knew she always wondered. "By the way, the forehead kisses… it's an impulse. It felt right. My mum always did the same when I was down. It felt… protective."

*I know,* Whisper thought, but the words that came out of her mouth offered Aaron the same respect to him, that he'd shown her.

"I felt the same from you. Every time you did it."


At the door, ready and with the door pushed open, Aaron turned. The light that leaked into the room highlighted Whisper as she stood in front of the couch. A brightness her room had never seen.

From behind the mask, she said, "See you next time I'm outside."

"Absolutely," Aaron replied. "See you out there, Whisper."

Nothing was out of the question when it came to what was sat behind the new door, but after worlds that almost ate him alive, events that rattled him, and constant unusual sights, Aaron knew it was his biggest step yet. With a deep breath to calm the shake in his legs, he once more crossed into an unfamiliar threshold and left Whisper and her newfound peace behind.

Met with a downward spiral of a staircase, Aaron's feet left ripples in the thin layers of blood that lined each step he trod.

The place was silent. Too silent, and as he got to the bottom of a staircase that just wouldn't let up, he noticed the huge brick-walled room he'd entered. It reminded him of an old church in the way it arched up over him. Minus the windows... here, they were merely gaps, where loose bricks had fallen and birthed an entrance for the light.

As he took a few more steps, the central pool took his gaze. Twice his height in diameter, the wall around it stood three feet tall. It was filled... almost overflowing with the same red liquid that painted the stairs and animated the door. Blood.

A hand touched his shoulder from behind and shot him into a spin until his face met hers.

And there she stood.
Rhiannon.

# 14

## RHIANNON

The left side of her body was flaking away in a disintegration caused by the sheer amount of weight that just her presence alone, caused. The crystallised remnants of the skin that was once whole, were blackened and decayed.

It floated, robbed of gravity. The side of her that remained whole was cracked, much like old porcelain, twinned with Whisper. Only the cracks in her skin were occupied by a white glow, rather than crimson. Head-to-

toe in a white gown, the left side of it, too, rotted away. She looked exactly like Rhian despite the obvious. Aaron almost reached out to hug her before he snapped into realisation.

"You're… Rhiannon?"

"I am," she said. The first voice on the island that perfectly reflected that of the woman he loves. The tone and the mannerisms were a perfect mirror.

With a simple gesture from her hand, she guided him to a bench that sat on the far side of the pool filled with blood. Aaron couldn't help but stare into the well as he walked past; his glitched reflection was all that stared back at him.

As they sat on it: a beautiful wood-seated cast iron bench that looked as though it had never been occupied before, Rhiannon sunk her head low until her chin met her chest. It seemed a lot of versions of Rhian had the same weight in their heads.

"What happened to you?" Aaron gazed upon her. He didn't mean to stare so… hard, but it was difficult not to.

"Life," she said. "Life, and all the memories it gave me." There was that word again. *Memories*.

"It looks like it's killing you."

"It is… slowly. It was always going to," she replied. She gazed at the fractured ceiling. "It's why I created Rhian."

*Created?* Aaron thought. He lingered on it as if it were the only word he knew. It dangled before his eyes on a thread and teased him.

"Rhian's not—she's not… Rhian?"

Rhiannon took to her cryptic side, much to the bother of Aaron. "She is… but she isn't," she said.

She lifted her head and turned it to Aaron. Immediately, she felt his confusion. Then she just looked blindly across the huge empty room, into nothing. The wind whistled as it pushed through the gaps and cracks in the walls that stared back. It pushed her hair into a dance with a light stroke.

"She is me, and I am her." She looked down to her feet. "Only I took from her everything that would have broken her…" She sniffled. "And I locked it all away."

"Memories," Aaron said. He knew exactly what she'd 'locked away.'

Rhiannon nodded. Every nod thrust the disconnected fragments of her cheek into an aimless float. Like dust, it lingered in the air.

The pool they sat against, rippled. A sharp, round jolt that pushed short waves from the inside to the out. The walls rumbled with it like something heavy and blunt had collided with them. Aaron watched as the liquid settled, patient in his curiosity. Minutes later, another… then another.

"So, what's doing *that*?" he asked. His eyes never moved from the unsettled puddle of red.

Rhiannon took a moment to answer, she really didn't want to. But she knew she had to. "She knows you're here," she whispered.

Brief was the answer he got, but an overflow of fear it held, too. *She,* as Rhiannon put it, had started to shake the very foundation of the island. Aaron asked Rhiannon what role exactly she played there. Her answer was short: she oversaw it all.

"The memories that cripple Rhian are mine," she explained. Aaron focused on every word she said. His ears were glued to her vocals.

"When I hid, a lifetime ago, from the demons that infested our mind... I created this place. I never meant to, I just sought to hide away from reality. Only I wasn't the only one."

Rhiannon moved her eyes to the top of the staircase Aaron had descended.

"The others... followed. Each with their own... flavours on the memories they kept."

She stood from the bench and looked at the deep pool of blood. Her eyes were lost, and her body was stiff as she stared into her own reflection.

"I – we exist so that she can forget." Like a possessed woman, only her head turned to meet Aaron. No motion left her neck or her shoulders, like her head spun on a separate axis. "But I fear that time has come to an end," she said.

Fear and worry passed through her words like spirits. Every quiver they left resonated with Aaron's soul as they clawed away at it. He stood with his arms tucked under each other against his chest. His shirt crumpled and creased under the fold.

"You think she's remembering, don't you?"

Rhiannon's eyes remained locked on him, then gently, they looked to his feet. She didn't have to say anything. It was one of 'those' looks.

"That's what's happening, right?" He picked through his memories. For once, they began to line up.

"Last night, or whenever it was, Rhian cycled. Every personality I've met on this island, all of them. She spat through them in an instant one by one until she couldn't breathe."

He pointed to the door that led him down. "Only none of those remember that. It wasn't them, was it?"

Rhiannon's head shook. "No."

As he wiped his face with cupped hands, desperate to pull away from the stress, Aaron surveyed the walls of the room. Another thunderous boom shook them. Aaron could taste the dust of the concrete as the vibration violently loosened the mortar between bricks like it was nothing.

"The nightmares, they're part of it. She said they weren't, but she was hiding from it." The words that slipped his mouth were supposed to be an inner thought.

His pupils shot side to side before they met Rhiannon again.

"She, Rhiannon. You said *she*."

She closed her eyes and viced her jaw. Her nose scrunched. "My mother," she scorned. "Lynn."

*Ember mentioned a Lynn*, Aaron thought. She'd said it was someone she knew.

"Lynn was your mother?" His eyebrows almost left a dent in the middle from how far they pointed to the bridge of his nose. "Why did nobody tell me that?"

His mind replayed what Stephanie slipped out: *Mummy didn't play nice.* Maybe in some way, one of them did. He just missed it.

"They weren't supposed to. They followed what they were told, mostly. The island is sacred. For you to be here…" She looked around. "I needed to be sure."

Aaron demanded more clarity; the brain could only handle so much guesswork.

"That you, Aaron, were as pure as her memories of you would suggest. The island is alive with Rhian and I, so the moment you stepped here… I knew. I needed to see what I felt she *knew*; that you were the missing piece in our chaotic world."

"Go on," he urged. This time, the information he was handed, needed to be clear. If anything, to save his mind from yet another meltdown.

Rhiannon moved to the edge of the bloody pool. She leant over slightly and dipped her index finger into it. The blood coated the tip of it, right to the first knuckle. With each name she reeled off, she'd score a mark in the single-brick ledge that surrounded it. A tally.

"Ember trusts nobody," she said. "Yet she took you to her fondest place. She opened up to you. Why?"

Aaron shrugged his shoulders as Rhiannon drew her first mark.

"Because not once did you treat her unequal. You treated her as a person. A real person. She felt welcomed in a world that was… against her. Because they saw her as an illness." She held her blood-dipped finger up as Aaron tried to speak.

"Dolly spent her entire existence here, hiding away from the memories that created her. She locked them away… but it messed with her fantasy. It fought back."

She drew her next red line in the brick.

"You brought out her true strength. She faced those memories and allowed them to be part of her. Because of you, nothing in her world is locked away from her."

The blood dried on her finger. She dipped it once more.

"Ma'am… Kathy," she said. "You helped her finish what she never could. Even I never knew you held the knowledge you did of her world, but, because you knew how to free her, you did just that. You took the time to invest in her freedom. Nothing stops her now. She's… free, to an extent."

"Hold on," Aaron interrupted. "If you never knew I'd seen The Sisters Three, then what *was* I supposed to do for Ma'am?"

A smirk crossed the face of the decaying woman. It cracked her lips open to show her bright teeth.

"Harmony." The word rolled off her tongue as smooth as silk. "Ma'am doesn't make friends easily, and she'd lost her only one on the outside. The opinion Rhian holds of you... well, let's just say it was a given that Ma'am would take to you."

"Hmph." That would have been easier, but Aaron held satisfaction in the knowledge that Ma'am was no longer stuck in a 'loop.' If he'd gotten the chance again, he wouldn't have done it any differently.

Rhiannon painted the next line.

"You showed Littlefoot that no matter how small you are, there's always an answer to the madness if you believe it. Now she sleeps unhindered in a place she's happy to call home."

Three lines quickly became four.

"Stephanie's opinion of the outside world is shifting—"

"Wait a minute," interrupted Aaron. I was sent to kill her. That's what 64 said."

Rhiannon laughed a little bit. "64 was never real, Aaron. Let's not forget, Stephanie removed the bow from her door, so you'd enter. She can make you see whatever she wants you to, we all can. She showed you only what people perceived her as; crazy and unstable."

Rhiannon looked through Aaron.

"Everybody she ever met was scared of her. Eager to shun her. Desperate for her to leave. She remembered that."

Rhiannon smiled. "She thought you, like them, wouldn't second guess an option to dispose of her, but you refused, didn't you?"

Aaron nodded. His brain had malfunctioned like a vintage computer. It was way too much to take in. He knew from the start that it all felt... rushed. He called it, multiple times.

"That's why everything went south the moment I walked in... it was planned to? Some attempt at what, directing me to whatever held them back?"

With a hint of shame, Rhiannon nodded. She did what she needed to and nothing less.

She continued, "You acknowledged that Stephanie was part of something you held close, and you *included* her in it. That's something she'd never seen." She dipped her finger once more. "You passed her test."

The fifth line presented itself on the brick, quickly followed by a sixth.

"Let me guess," said Aaron. A faint scoff as he figured it out. "I helped Whisper by giving her a way to shut out her demons." He was so proud of himself, chest puffed out and head inflated.

"No," said Rhiannon. The smile swept away from Aaron's face.

Rhiannon's eyes lifted with her soul as she told him. "You helped Whisper by staying with her… *after* the door had appeared. You didn't leave until she was ready for you to. The voices that told her you would go… you proved them wrong."

The ground shook once more. A crack formed in the wall of the pool. Blood began to leak in a steady stream between it. Flakes of bricks in the walls around them fell like crumbs onto the floor with a gentle sprinkle and supporting girders began to creak and moan.

"This…" Rhiannon lifted her eyes and her palms to face the ceiling and looked around. "Rhian being here, it was always going to happen. It just needed to be the right time, around the right people. Felix, bless his heart, passed his time onto you, and when it came to be, you were right where you should have been. Right by her side as the universe beckoned it"

Aaron had to lift his jaw shut with his hand. He'd known the convenience of it all, but not to that extent. He felt like the puppet to Rhiannon's puppeteer. "So, I'm this… *missing piece?* For what?" For a moment, his question was unanswered. A memory that masked itself as ignorance.

"You know, I counted them," Rhiannon whimpered as she took a few steps back from the well. "The beatings."

Aaron almost felt as broken as the woman in front of him looked. The cracks in her voice and the quake in her legs translated what she felt in perfect clarity.

"They never stopped. I was born to be here. But Rhian wasn't, and if we both remain…" she pointed to the crack that had formed in the well. "The whole world we've created will crack, just like that. Until there is nothing left. You don't want to know what happens when that does."

Another thud fluttered the world. This time it stuck around for longer. The crack in the pool grew bigger and the stream of blood turned into a forced gush. It was like a valve had been opened that just pushed it all through.

"You know where she is." Aaron could see it on Rhiannon's face. There's no way she'd go through all she'd explained if she didn't.

Rhiannon's cheeks paled more. Like a ghost had taken a hold of them. "She's in the pit," she said, with a stiff nod.

Aaron gulped. Whisper had spoken of the pit. Of what was there. "She's with the monster?" he shuddered.

Another nod returned to him as a tear fell down Rhiannon's pained face. Then another rumble, massive. On a scale much bigger than any before. It felt like the whole building was going to fall on top of Aaron in a million pieces. The crack in the pool grew so big the blood practically fell out of it and lined the floor.

"How do I finish this?" Aaron begged.

"None of us know exactly what this missing piece is you're supposed to play, Aaron. But now it's time to find out."

Rhiannon thrust her arms out and closed her eyes tight shut. With what Aaron considered 'magic,' and a strained look upon her face, she summoned a door behind him. Just a normal, wooden house door with a silver handle.

"I hope you're ready," she said as she passed a large key into Aaron's open palm. It came from nowhere, like it just appeared, and was, without question, the heaviest key he'd ever held. Black jewels lined the head of it in the pattern of a skull. The body of the key - scratched and aged silver that looked older than the world it belonged to.

Aaron glanced at it. "Ready for what?" he asked.

"The truth of how we came to be. The *real* truth. And if you make it far enough, I pray that you find Rhian. It's not too late, I can feel her. Don't hesitate, just get on the boat, and your part will play out, as it's supposed to. Whatever that looks like…"

Aaron returned his gawp sharp to Rhiannon. She made as much sense as the cryptic answers she loved to give him. "What do you mean if I make it far-"

Rhiannon slung the door open with a hurricane-like wind and whipped Aaron through it as the air circled around him like a gigantic hand.

As the door slammed shut, another rumble battered the roof. Tiles and gutters slammed against the floor around Rhiannon as the structure began to fret. She walked back over to the bench… and sat. There was nothing more she could do, except wait for the end and hope it was the one she craved.

"Please, Aaron, help undo my thievery," she cried. "So that I can finally be free."

# 15
## MEMORY LANE

The dock, as Aaron remembered it… almost. It was a flash in time as he saw himself back there, only it was clear of any mist and obstruction, and a boat lay next to it like a welcome mat… it wasn't there before. Not in his first visit, nor in his brief return when he explored it further.

Aaron was back where his journey started, what felt like a week ago, at the cold lake. The air didn't feel quite as bitter this time, but somehow, Aaron still found a shiver within him.

As instructed, he wasted no time and sat in the small wooden boat. There was no oar or paddle in sight, but instead, a mind of its own. It moved slowly across the waters and pushed every fallen leaf out of the way as it sliced through. Everything was calm. A nice break from the madness.

As the boat sailed to its destination, Aaron inspected the key Rhiannon had given him. The imprint lay as clear in his hand as the key itself. Forked twin prong teeth, the jewelled skull that made the head of it. It was odd, like some form of a relic. He had no more time to ogle the artifact, however. His ride stopped and tucked right at the bottom of a towering staircase. One that wrapped around the tall building which once peeked its head above the clouds. Aaron remembered the multiple times he'd asked himself what the building could be, and now he was about to find out.

*I suppose I'd better get started*, Aaron thought.

His foot slipped a clumsy inch as it pressed against the damp wood, his second the same. With that in mind, he took narrow strides to the first step. Up and up, he went, past the line of the lowest cloud.

At the top of his ascension, Aaron was met with a rusted metal door. Like something that should have been slapped at the entrance to a bunker. Ma'am had a similar one, only hers sported fewer scratches, rust, and dents. A dominant rusted-yellow sign hung from slagged and worn rope that met with his eyes. Bold black lettering cautioned him with a shout.

DO NOT ENTER

"Well, that's comforting," Aaron muttered.

He slid the key into its home, and with a swift click to the left, the door sprung open. Like it was happy to be unlatched. What stood before Aaron next, threw his mind into a warp.

Charcoal smoke span in a ring, counterclockwise, and spat sparks in its rotation. An alive centre mass that wriggled around, reminded him of Rhiannon's door, only it spun in the opposite direction of the ring that surrounded it. It defied... everything. Nothing else was there. An empty, cramped room like you'd find at the peak of a lighthouse. A blank canvas with this... thing just stood in the centre of it, that stared at Aaron. The sight of it alone invited doubt as Aaron wondered if he should enter it.

It didn't look like there was anything else to do, so he bit the inside of his lower lip so hard it almost drew blood and pushed out a soft growl as he walked through.

"Please don't swallow me," he said. Then in the blink of an eye, he was in another room.

It was a bedroom. One he recognised.

Dirty walls, a stained single bed with the sheets in a ruffle. A sticker of a large pink hot air balloon. A thin set of drawers with a broken tv sat on top. Three bears lined on the floor, in the same pink that painted the balloon. Curtainless, mould-laced windows that leaked naked daylight into the room onto the bloodstained, tatty carpet. Something out of a horror movie.

This time, Aaron stood usual-sized within it as he left the… portal. He witnessed it all in one single sharp image.

A young brown-haired girl sat up against the head of the bed. She sobbed her broken little heart out so hard it juddered the breaths she tried to take between them. On closer inspection, her eye was swollen, ready to bruise, and her lip was cut. Blood dribbled down her chin with the saliva she'd lost.

Her lovely pink pyjamas were tainted by the blood that dripped down onto them. Aaron couldn't watch any more of it. The longer he did, the more his heart collapsed inside of him, it wasn't in his nature to just ogle it.

He picked up the bears from the floor in a huddle and sat beside the girl, just at her feet.

"Here," he said. He lined the bears beside her leg. "These will protect you."

The child stayed in her sob; she couldn't control it. Between the breaths she struggled to hold, she cried, "Thank you."

He didn't ask her name. He already knew it; it was obvious who the young girl was. Sick to his stomach, Aaron struggled to leave the room and descended the stairs that had formed directly outside it. They weren't there before; he knew because they were exactly where he'd entered the room.

The next room he found himself in was no better.

A woman sat casually on the two-seated sofa. The disgusting dirty red rag of a shirt she wore barely fit her properly. A little bit overweight, she smelt like an ashtray and sat with a beer bottle in one hand and a cigarette in another.

Aaron recognised the sofa as the filthy cream one he'd hidden under in Littlefoot's world. The living room, too. No carpet lay among the floor, just bare concrete as though any carpet that was there before had been ripped clean up. They'd probably sold it on for drugs, or beer.

The woman's greasy, unkept mop of a hairstyle flopped onto the folds of her neck. The crease of the arm that held her beer, was decorated with bruised pinholes. Three of them. A druggie. It would explain the syringes that lay carefree on the floor. They were just as vile then as they were up-close. Aaron would know.

The woman *had* to be Lynn.

A child, unmistakable as the same child he'd met in the bedroom, screamed her heart out in the background.

Not a sob, a scream. One that perfectly announced the presence of a child who wasn't looked after properly. Cries that would panic any parent... those of torture and heartbreak.

The mess of a woman that slouched without care, drowned out the screams with her beer and cigarettes. Unlike young Rhian did, moments ago, Lynn never saw Aaron. Like a ghost in the night, he was just... there... watching. He turned around, away from the addict, and another staircase awaited him at the opposite door; the door he'd entered the room from in Littlefoot's world. It led him to another floor.

He was back in the living room. Was there a mistake?

Four people, including the untidy woman from the couch, stood in the middle of the room. They surrounded the cluttered coffee table and filled the room with shouts. They argued about who would buy the next 'stash,' and Lynn was adamant it couldn't be her because she had to look after her 'bastard of a child.'

The words she slung from her mouth struck Aaron like a spear. Straight through his chest as his heart practically beat itself apart. He knew exactly who that referred to. Aaron looked down, just through the left of his eyes. Two small, unwashed bare feet at the bottom, were just about visible in the shadow behind the sofa. They caught his attention. Attached to them, young

Rhian, as she hid away from the noises, intimidated and scared.

Aaron leant his body down until his head came into her view. He held his hand out; he was going to get her out of there whether he was allowed to or not.

"Take my hand," he ushered in a soft voice. "It's okay, I promise I won't hurt you."

Young Rhian reached her own hand until it clutched his and Aaron pulled her with a gentle tug until she raised to her feet. Her hands quivered so heavy that they rattled his arms.

Past the obviously drug-riddled bullies, he snuck Rhian. It was a surprise they never saw them leave. Out of the room, they went, through the far door and across the hallway until Rhian was safe in her own room. The same, bloodied, stained embarrassment of a child's bedroom. He picked her up and placed her softly on the bed. Her feet kicked with anxiety as she watched him pick her bears up off the floor. She didn't know this man, so didn't know if he would hurt her, too.

"You remember these three, right?" He asked.

She nodded. Of course, she did know them.

"Good," he said. He placed them by her side and faced all three toward her. "Stay with them for me."

He noticed the uncertainty on her face.

"They helped me take down a big balloon with lasers for turrets, you know."

Young Rhian looked at the bears, then back to Aaron with wide eyes.

"That's right, they're *super* strong. They'll protect you." He wiped a tear that fell from her eye to her cheek and rested his hand on the back of her small head. "You'll be okay."

Then he gently squeezed her upper arm. "Yep, just as I figured. *You're* pretty strong too," he joked. Somehow the little girl managed to summon the smallest of smiles.

Young Rhian hugged her bears, and Aaron switched on her tv so she could drown out the noise that invaded from across the hall. Of course, The Sisters Three began to play. He recognised the theme tune anywhere. It drew a smile on his otherwise troubled face.

"They'll protect you too," he said as he pointed to the tv. Then he left the room, not that he wanted to, and not without a couple of looks back to the child.

As if it were a pattern, right outside Rhian's room was the next staircase that led him down once more, and to somewhere startlingly different.

A... diner?

90's era music played through tinny speakers. Dishes clattered and hot oil sizzled as it cooked some of the best smelling burgers Aaron had ever graced his nose with. Booths littered from the front to the back in two symmetrical lines. The booths at the far sides curled under the windows and capped both ends in comfortable cream leather. It was some old static caravan that had been extended and converted.

The central counter stood like a kitchen island as two adults sat there. Lynn, and a strange man in a white vest. Another familiar sight. Aaron crept through the pristine white and black checkerboard tiled floor, dodged booths, and forced stealth. As he walked past Lynn and her man, Aaron wished he'd had his ears sewn shut.

"No, Graham, and she ain't havin' anythin' either!" Lynn snapped.

Graham laughed, almost hard enough to shake the dirt that rode his skin. He was a gold standard, run of the mill, textbook crackhead. The snort his laugh forced made Aaron want to punch him in his blackened teeth. "Yeah, more for us," he scoffed. "Get rid of her."

Clearly, his insult was aimed at young Rhian.

"Like I haven't bloody tried, Graham. Stuck with her ain't i. Ungrateful little bitch."

Aaron held back the urge to slam their faces into the food that sat on their plates; it would have been a waste of the double-stacked burgers. He looked around the diner and hoped Rhian was there, somewhere.

Then…over, hidden in a booth, her two little bare feet poked out as she parked her back against a window and held her head down to her chest. The same unwashed feet that hid under the sofa.

Aaron looked at the corner of the crumpled newspaper next to Lynn's mess of a presence.

MAY 14<sup>TH</sup> – 1993

He swiped a blue-iced chocolate muffin from the neatly presented straw basket next to it and took it with him as he walked over to Rhian. He just *knew* she hadn't been fed.

"Hey," he whispered as he stood next to the booth. His voice was different to what the child was used to. It sounded... calm. Nice, even. She stole a glance at him as she played with her hands, and all the beatings she'd ever received projected from her eyes and into Aaron's. His breath shook at the slip of his sympathy, but he masked it with a friendly smile.

"I just wanted to give you this."

Rhian's eyes widened with delight as she snatched the cake Aaron placed on the table. She dug into it like she hadn't eaten in days. No crumb or speck was wasted in the wide-jawed bites she took. A hungry, underfed child that wept with every delicious, blueberry flavoured mouthful.

Aaron looked down. "Happy Birthday, kid," he said as he walked away.

The next set of steps he were to take, appeared right where he'd walked in. He was lost in exactly how their spawns worked and just strapped in for the ride.

Fourteen steps took him down another level.

# 16
## MEMORIES AFLAME

He counted the floors. He'd made his way to the fifth. Aaron's attention was immediately snatched as Lynn's kitchen came into view.

"Ungrateful little bitch!" she snapped. Clearly, that was her favourite insult when it came to her daughter. Hollow thuds and child's screams soon followed. Lynn had lashed into the young girl.

"Who said you could eat that?"

Rhian's voice trembled as she begged for mercy. "Please, I'm hungry!"

The begs and pleads did nothing as Lynn thrashed fist and palm into a defenceless Rhian.

Aaron filled with adrenaline as he stood in the doorway. Rhian or not, it didn't sit well. He ran as fast as he could to the disgusting display of abuse and dragged Lynn away with a single arm wrapped around her waist. He yanked her like he'd pulled the rope of a chainsaw. To his surprise, it worked. She shot across the kitchen five feet until she collided with the sink so firm it bent her backwards.

The child lay on the floor, her eye swollen, ready to bruise. Blood dripped from her lower lip and started to leak onto her pyjamas. Aaron guessed that had he not intervened, he'd have found Rhian sitting on her bed, sobbing instead.

Surprised that he could interact with Lynn, Aaron stood protective over Rhian. Lynn wouldn't get past his blockade. He held his hands above his head.

"I don't want any trouble," he said. "Just leave her alone, please."

Lynn yelled from deep in her chest with a growl, like an animal. "Grant!"

Moments later, a stocky, beer-bellied, dirty tracksuit wearing man walked into the kitchen from the living room. His hair was so thin it revealed the spot-ridden scalp that sat below it.

*Great,* thought Aaron. *Another crackhead.*

Grant charged at Aaron as if he were a bull, and Aaron had waved the muleta.

Sure to prevent anything from landing anywhere near Rhian, Aaron wrestled with Grant. He wasn't a fighter, so Grant easily overpowered him and threw an array of punches. They hit him hard in the face, but as long as it was him, and not the girl, he made peace with it. For a druggie, Grant had quite some steam. Then again, maybe it was fuelled by the drugs that ran through his protruding veins.

Aaron closed his eyes and let it happen, then, after a few everlasting moments, it came to a stop. The noise, the impacts, all of it just… ceased. Aaron opened his eyes, slow with caution as he expected more hits to follow.

Instead, Rhian stood over him and looked down.

"You're bleeding," she said. Then she passed him a tissue. Aaron thanked her.

"I'll survive." He wiped the blood that trickled from his nose. "Are you okay?"

Young Rhian nodded. It threw her hair into a bounce as it sat on her shoulders. "I'm Rhiannon," she said.

Aaron smiled at the sound of the name. "I'm Aaron." And with a wink, he said, "That's a nice name you've got."

The relief Aaron felt, in knowing he'd protected her, swept through the room like a monsoon. He tucked his ribs as he stood back up, barely able to stand straight. It felt like the ribs he held didn't even exist anymore.

He winked, best he could from his swollen eye. "Glad you're okay."

As he limped away, toward the next steps that beckoned him down, right where the door should be, he muttered, "I won't let them hurt you." He didn't know it was loud enough that the young girl had heard it.

They led to a door, the next flight of steps. Just a simple door, like Aaron had opened many times thus far. It was a white door, scarred by scuffs and marks. At this point, doors were a nuisance to him. He kicked it open as he rocked his body back, then hobbled through.

Stood outside a random bungalow he'd never seen before, the obvious sound of sirens pulled him further down the street he'd entered.

Thick smoke bellowed above another bungalow as he approached it. A bungalow Aaron recognised from Littlefoot's world. Neighbours stood around in chatter and gasped among themselves. Like a flock of pigeons over spilt food, they just littered the street in a crowded gathering.

Then Aaron saw what they were mid-gawp of. Lynn stood central to the overgrown grass garden at the front of the bungalow. She held Rhian by the scruff of her neck, faced away from everybody, drunk beyond comprehension and oblivious to it all. She slammed her hand into Rhian's face so hard it threw her from the grip, and she hit the ground with a soft thud.

Aaron's eyes teared up as he froze. He'd begun to understand the pain that Rhian, or *Rhiannon*, had endured those years ago. He knew now, more than Rhian herself had remembered.

An older fellow that stood to his left, turned to Aaron. "Kid's gonna grow up with all kinds of issues," he remarked. The ignorance was foul.

Aaron flared his nostrils and shot his face to within an inch of the man's. "Let's just hope one of them isn't standing around doing nothing when a child is in danger, eh?!" he barked.

The sirens that wailed in the background grew louder and louder. Lynn grabbed the helpless Rhian by her collar and dragged her inside the smoke engulfed bungalow, three sheets to the wind and ignorant to everything that was in development behind them.

Aaron never wasted a single moment. He covered his mouth and nose with the collar of his t-shirt and paced for the door they entered. Into a nightmare pit of smoke and heat.

He found himself back inside the living room within the first few steps he took. Like he was pulled there. Only the home wasn't ablaze yet. Lynn was passed out on the couch. A cigarette had fallen from her lazy hand and landed among the rubbish that littered the floor. The flames it created began to climb up the sofa like a spider would ascend its thread.

Rhian stood there, watching. She didn't know what to do, so she shook at her mother's arm and begged her to wake. A series of shouts and shoves.

"Mommy. Mommy, wake up!"

Eventually, it stirred Lynn. She shot to her feet faster than Aaron thought she had it in her to.

She looked at the fire that began to grow beside her, then grabbed Rhian's shoulders. Like she was nothing but a cheap plastic toy, she shook her so hard it juddered her jaw.

"You little bitch! What have you done?!"

"It wasn't her!" Aaron shouted, but it was unheard. Another memory where he was unseen and unable to help.

Rhian escaped from Lynn's clutches with a thrash of her small arms and ran for the door. Aaron followed but was blinded by a flash of smoke that jammed his vision like an emp to a camera. As he opened his eyes, he was in Rhian's bedroom once more. Like he'd missed an entire part of his journey, he was just... there now.

Rhian was sat on the bed while she played with her bears.

"Aargh! Be careful of the pink ship of doom!" she playfully acted. Laser noises spat from her mouth as her bears took enemy fire. "Yes Ma'am," she replied to herself in a lower, grumbled tone. The television was on in the background. It was the final episode of The Sisters Three where Ma'am and her sisters were amid the trenches, desperate to avoid the Zeppelin above.

Rhian's re-enactment was adorable but soon interrupted when smoke began to flood her room. Thick with dust and full of fumes that attacked her throat and forced a weighted choke.

Aaron turned to the door it came through and got a nice up-close look at the smoke as it slapped him in the face. It cleared with the wave of his hands, but he found himself in yet another room. The constant switch of location and time began to make him feel uneasy.

A wall of fire blocked him from the doorway to the kitchen. Through the heated orange flickers, he could see Lynn, hands wrapped once again where they should never be... around Rhian's throat. She hurled abuse and diverted blame as only she knew how.

"Your little plan backfired, didn't it missy! If I die, you die. That what you want?!"

Rhian begged for her life. Her voice drowned in the tears that wouldn't stop.

"You little swine!" Lynn raised her hand to swipe the child but a chunk of the broken ceiling, the size of a thick magazine dropped onto her shoulder and knocked her down. It gave Rhian the time she needed to run as fast as her little legs would take her.

Aaron wanted to make sure Rhian got to safety, but it wasn't so easy. Blocked by the fire, he had no choice but to run through the exit, where his aim was the back garden.

As he got outside, young Rhian ran from the back gate that was held open by overgrown shrubbery in the jungle-like garden. She nearly tripped over the uneven slabs that flicked up beneath her tiny feet. She didn't know where to look as she made it out. Was it the strange man that stood on the grass and watched her, or the crowd of strangers that bordered around her?

Loud, obnoxious sirens screamed as three fire engines and two ambulances pulled into the street. One particular fireman made a b-line for Rhian as she stood on the grass. Through no fault of his own, he wasn't quick enough to catch her when she collapsed in a bloodied daze onto the soft green beneath her feet.

The fireman picked her up in a steady lift and carried her to safety, and as two others passed him, in a hefty British accent he said, "Dunno if there's anyone else inside mate, have a check will ya?"

Aaron's jaw formed a gap as it dropped an inch. He only knew one other person with a British accent *that* thick. He watched idly by as the fireman placed Rhian on the back step of an ambulance that parked with its back facing the bungalow.

"You're alright, kid. We gotcha," he said.

In a monumental wave of heat that rushed Aaron's bloodstream, like boiled water, he too, almost collapsed as he watched it all play out.

His glossed eyes looked back to the ambulance, back to the little girl that sat on the step. She'd fitted with an oxygen mask. "What did she do to you?" he whispered.

His ears pulled him back to his left as Lynn stormed from the bungalow, in an alcohol-induced rage of yells and shouts.

"Rhiannon, where'd ya go you little shit?!" She made it not even ten feet before her drunken eyes saw the flash of lights and the swarm of gossip-hungry civilians. Every single one of them looked upon her in disgust.

"What?" she snorted. She finished her beer in a single swig and smashed the bottle against the side of her home with a lousy launch.

She saw the uniforms that surrounded Rhian as she sat at the back of the ambulance. Police, a fireman, and paramedics. The police presence alone was enough to scare her. She guessed her time was up, and as towered flames three times her height ripped through the bungalow, she walked straight back into it without a second thought. The fire swallowed her like she was nothing. To Lynn, that was easier than admitting what she'd done to her daughter.

Rhian sat and watched it all happen. Frozen stiff, she stared at the doorway as her mother willingly walked into the fire. She hated the woman and yet still, a fresh tear formed in her eye, just moments before she passed out.

Aaron remained in his place like a statue for ten minutes. Everything became a blur to him as he tried to register the new levels of pain he'd unlocked. Through it all, he told himself, imagine what *she* felt. Imagine years of endless pain at the hands of someone you loved through it all.

The tears that streamed down his face had dried into a line of stickiness that parted the dust and dirt. His veins ran as cold as the air in his lungs, and his skin became pale and riddled with tiny bumps. His chest was nothing but a vessel for his heart to relentlessly strike against, and his feet were overthrown by an invasion of numbness. All the while his fists were clenched, and his jaw was locked. The multiple ribs he'd broken, and the inflation of his eye seemed like nothing in comparison to it all.

Three identical, wooden knocks yanked him from his daze. It spun his head smart until it met the door that had appeared behind him.

*Not another door,* he thought. He was done with them now, fully.

Still, he stepped to it and remained shaken. The wood of it was warm to the touch which was unusual.

He'd seen it before, the door. It was the one that led him to this… nightmare. The white door that had chips and scuffs all over it. All Aaron knew, was that wherever it led, it had to be better than what he just witnessed. Anything would be, but just one thought crept in front of the rest.

Was this the final door, or another that led to another which led to yet another?

The handle hissed as he touched it. He snatched his hand away and stopped the profanity that was eager to spill out of him. He shook his hand against the cold air and tried again.

The heat that swam from the door as he opened it threw him off balance as it wrapped around him like a blanket. Nevertheless, it was a door. He treated it as such and walked through with the hope that it was the last time he'd have to.

# 17

# FIRESTARTER

B eads of sweat trickled down Aaron's face with every step he took down another spiralled staircase that seemed to mirror what he'd scaled to the top of the tower. The source of the heat grew closer and closer as he traversed into oblivion.

As the heat ramped from warm to hot, down over the balustrade, the bright pit of fire thrashed and spat. It was violent and unstable, like a sea in stormy weather. It bubbled like a jacuzzi from its centre, only one you would never want to step near, let alone *in.* The lower the steps took him, the more deadly it all seemed to Aaron.

An object stuck out as the fire flickered its light against it. A cage. It sat isolated against the far wall of a room that mirrored Rhiannon's. The only thing that accompanied the cage was the pool of heat.

A cage in which it seemed someone sat in, huddled in the corner. A woman. One which Aaron had searched high and low for, for an impossible length of time. The woman he loved more than anyone or anything else on the planet. Aaron's heart skipped a beat. He pushed his back foot firm into the steps and launched himself down them with a force that nearly toppled him over. He raced down and shot straight for the cage as he called her name.

She was unconscious, it looked like. Once Aaron skidded his body to the floor and started to clang away at the rusty bars of the cage, he didn't rest until her body moved. Slight, yet clear, it soon did.

Rhian heard the commotion. "Aaron?" Her eyes took time to adjust to the bright light the pit of fire opposite her shone upon the room. The grid pattern shadow it cast over her trapped her own shadow in another prison.

"Yeah, it's me," said Aaron.

"How?" Rhian didn't believe what she heard, or faintly saw for even a second. Her mind had a habit of playing tricks on her, she wouldn't have put it past this being another.

"That's a *really* long story. I'm here now. Right in front of you."

Rhian began to simper. Her eyes leaked and her head dropped low. "Leave me alone," she cried.

A rumble startled them both. It shook the room and rattled the stairs. The central pit of fiery doom began to thrash harder. Aaron didn't even have to inhale to smell the heat.

"Hey, Rhian, it's me. I promise, no tricks."

Rhian cried harder. Aaron had to think. Then he picked up a small stone from beside him and reached his arm a foot into the cage. He scratched something into the floor with it and when he was done, he called Rhian's name again and waited until she saw it.

She turned, slow. She looked down upon the floor of her prison and read his message.

WESTERNS > PERIODS

Was that a smile that cracked from her misery, or was it a hallucination spawned of Aaron's hope? Whichever it was, it lasted but a mere fraction of a second before Rhian convinced herself she had been lied to, again. She tested him.

"Did you know," she asked. "About everything I didn't."

Sweat fell from Aaron's head into an ever-growing puddle on the floor. It leaked to the knees he had planted against it. "No. I didn't, not until I came here. You know I'd tell you otherwise."

Rhin sank into a deeper sob as she pushed her back against the side of the cage. It almost sang a symphony in the howls she cried. "Why did she hate me so much?" The words fell through her tears like she'd held onto them for too long.

Much apparent was the obvious; Rhian now had full access to the memories she was once protected from. *She*, referred to Lynn once more.

"Lynn? Some people are just that ugly in life. You deserved none of it. Trust me, I've seen it all."

Rhian's doubt was as clear as day. In both her eyes and her face as she lifted them. "I'm a murderer."

It was such a strong word, and Aaron was quick to argue her use of it. But Rhian wouldn't have any of it.

Her deep inhales dragged a chord with them as her throat seized shut. "I watched her. She – I watched as she went back, and I just let her burn. I'm… I'm a monster."

Her sob became uncontrollable. It reminded Aaron of how broken and hurt her cries as a child were.

"Hey!" He banged his hand against the cage. Through everything he'd seen, not one single thing proved her case.

"Listen to me. You're no monster, Rhian. Get that out of your head, right now. I wouldn't come all this way and see all I did, to be sitting here if I thought any of it made you a monster, would I?"

Rhian just stared through her tears, still startled from his shout.

"Would I?" he reinforced.

She shook her head in question as her eyebrows dropped. Aaron's voice coiled back from his shout in favour of a softer delivery.

"Lynn made her bed. Years of throwing you around and beating you… that was going to catch up to her eventually. She chose that over facing what she'd done and left you to watch helplessly from the back of that ambulance. She took the coward's way out."

He leaned his head closer to the bars until he could see her clearly, and her, him.

"Something you would *never* do."

A reflection from the flicker of orange light danced in Rhian's eyes as they stared deep at Aaron. She was transfixed, her mind elsewhere. Her lips pursed as she tried to say something, but she lost it. Then she found other words.

"How do you know so much about that day?" Again, she was convinced it was a trick. Only she knew that, and she'd not long remembered it.

Aaron didn't leave her words waiting.

"I saw it all. Probably in a similar way you remembered it, Rhian. I was there while it played out like a movie." He rubbed his swollen eye. "A very… physical movie."

Rhian needed to know it was all real. She pulled herself to her knees and crawled forward through the cramped cage until she sat just inches away from him. The terror in her eyes put the same in Aaron's as she poked her arm through the bars and stroked the swelling that replaced his eye. It smudged the tracks his tears had left.

"What did you do?" she asked.

Aaron shook his head. "Nothing I wouldn't do again if it meant I could bring you home."

She smiled at him. Her hand sat lower to the side of his face and rested there. "You can't save me, Aaron. Nobody can."

He knew he couldn't. It only took a goofy doctor, seven worlds and a road trip through hell to realise it, but Aaron became aware that he couldn't save Rhian.

"I know." His head bowed. "It's a running theme, I guess. But… there's also another-"

Aaron didn't find time to finish what he'd started to say when another rumble boxed his aching ribs. The pit of fire began to escalate as the thrashes collided with one another.

"Screw this." He turned to his right and picked up the largest stray rock he saw. It sat in his hand like a brick. With a deep breath and a wind up stacked with pressure, he slammed it down onto the chain that strapped the cage door to its latch.

Rhian sprung her arm back inside it and took shelter back into the corner.

"No," she fretted. She repeated it fast, ten times in half the seconds. Aaron's eyes narrowed as he followed her cower.

"You shouldn't have done that," she whimpered.

"Why not? I'm trying to get you out of here."

The fear in Rhian's voice made Aaron look at the rock in his hand. Then the chain he'd pulled from the cage. He couldn't figure out what was so bad about it.

Then Rhian spoke two single words that threw him off-kilter.

"She's awake."

*Who*? Aaron thought. Then he followed Rhian's eyes with the rumble of the room, as they scaled upward, and her body sank. She begged for Aaron to run. Instead, he turned.

To his horror, from the cesspool of fire rose a gigantic figure. Up high, it stood until it reached its maximum. Twenty feet above the man who couldn't believe what he saw.

It burned head to toe like a statue born of lava and spat steaming lumps of rock, the size of tennis balls onto the floor below. A couple of which, just narrowly missed Aaron.

Rhian continued to beg and plead, but he came this far… Aaron didn't intend on leaving her behind. "Let's run!" But Rhian didn't plan on it.

Even if the metal that surrounded her weren't there, she'd have still been locked in her prison of fear. All she wanted was for Aaron to leave so he wouldn't get hurt. At the same time, to her annoyance, she knew just how stubborn he could be when it came to her.

*He's going to get himself killed!* She thought. "Aaron, just go! Now!"

Instead, he stood at the mercy of the flame-born giant. As his eyes ogled it, he spoke to Rhian.

"We both know who that is. Goes without saying. Rhian, you have to stand your ground, you can't let her drag you down. Look where that's led you. I know how strong you are, and this isn't it."

No reply returned to him as Rhian was frozen stiff. Unconvinced by his words, she was ready to slap the daft out of him.

"I just wish there was a way you could see that," he said as he looked back at her.

"*You* are in control, not her. For Christ's sake, Rhian, this is *your* world!"

A fusion of vex and worry was all that he could see on the woman he pleaded with. He sighed and looked back to the monster that loomed above him.

"That's right," he snarled. "You. A big, steaming pile of nothing! You did this to her. Lynn, right?"

The giant growled. It vibrated the walls.

Rhian had no idea what to do. What the hell was Aaron playing at?

"You're disgusting." He hurled as much abuse at the flamed embodiment of Lynn as he heard her throw at young Rhian many times over. "I saw what you did to that little girl. I saw how you treated her. Walking into that fire was hands down the _best_ thing you could have ever done."

Another growl as Lynn lowered her head to Aaron until it sat just ten feet above him. The heat was aggressive.

Rhian mustered another broken plea to ears that didn't receive it.

Aaron's voice began to break. "You should have been protecting her. Like I protect her, and she protects m-"

Aaron dropped his gaze to the floor. Inside that trampled brain of his, something ticked away. Something big. And that was it…

Rhian was protective of Aaron. He remembered how she stroked his poorly eye, and how she'd always nurse him when he was ill. He remembered how Ember helped him up the embankment, how Dolly pulled him away from the barrier. Ma'am carted him through the trenches to safety, Littlefoot saved him from the bird. Wherever there was a chance, he was the one being saved by her. He'd go as far as to say that meeting Rhian at that concert, saved him from a life without her. He was that grateful for her. He took note of the words his mind spoke. They were clear.

*Maybe she just needs a little push in the right direction.* He smiled. But was a smile that just reeked of trouble. He gathered Lynn's attention once more.

"Hey!"

A growl bellowed. She lowered further. Just feet above him. The heat that surrounded her curled the hair of Aaron's thin beard.

"You never deserved to be called a mother. Not if that word meant trading love for anything you could do to stick a needle in your arm."

Lynn turned her scorched head to Rhian as she cried in her cage. She watched, helpless as Aaron lectured her demon.

"Look at me!" Aaron roared.

He pointed his finger stiff to Lynn as she turned back. "Unlike you, I know who Rhian is. Unlike you, my love for her isn't decided by the mood I'm in or how much money I can get from it. And unlike you, I could *never* see her hurt."

Aaron stole another look across his left, to the cage where Rhian sat and gulped. The look he shared just told her he was going to do something stupid. She clutched at the bars and howled one last plea. A plea that echoed through the demented room for an age. A plea that was shunned, but not through ignorance… through a daring plan.

Aaron cracked his neck, took a breath, and stared into the eyes of his lover's abuser.

"Hey, Lynn," he shouted. "Fuck you, you ungrateful… little… bitch!"

The roar that followed could pop ears. It spawned a vibration so intense that nothing felt secure, not even the ground beneath Aaron. Wood, metal, and brick all rattled like they were loose at the joins. The giant monster wound her arm back, and it cooled into a solid limb of rock. Aaron clenched his eyes shut in wait and Lynn swung hard against his side. It took forever for the impact to land, but when it did, it slung Aaron far across the other side of the pit and slammed him into the wall. His limp body just thudded against the floor with no resistance.

"Nooooooo!" Rhian's throat nearly ripped itself to pieces as she kicked the door of the cage open and ran as fast as she could to Aaron.

But Aaron wasn't out for the count just yet. Heavily injured and his head bloodied from the gash the collision caused, he mustered himself into a seated position and waited for the next blow.

"Do it," he coughed. "Prove me right."

Lynn raised her massive hand for a second swipe, but Rhian stopped her as she paced dead ahead of

Aaron. She blocked the path of the strike, and the monster stopped in its tracks.

"Stop!" yelled Rhian.

Then Lynn swung her arm back again. She didn't care that Rhian stood in her way, it only strengthened the intent.

"Go ahead, try me," Rhian said, with her eyes alone.

Nothing. Lynn froze. It was clear she shared a look with Rhian. Something sat within the young woman's eyes that threw her demon off.

A barrage of memory and emotion hit Rhian like a freight train. "Remind me of how that felt. Do it! Remind me of how you broke me!"

A soft groan came from the giant. It backed up a step within its pool. It retreated just enough that Rhian began to realise the power that sat in her words.

Rhian had more to say through her cries as she pointed to the cage that she'd busted open. "You know, I sat there, forever, and I asked myself over and over again, why I would have watched you burn that way. Why I didn't shout your name or why I never ran after you." She sniffed her tears back and stood tall.

"YOU WOULD NEVER HAVE DONE THE SAME FOR ME!"

Aaron was thrown back by how loud Rhian's shouts became. He'd never, *never* seen so much hatred and anger on her. It dressed her head to toe in a thick dose.

He remained mute on purpose; he didn't want to trigger her any more than she already was. He knew she had the situation under control.

Lynn began to shrink from her massive figure until she stood no more than fifteen feet tall, but Rhian was far from done. She'd open the floodgates to a lifetime of hard truths.

"So, you, and your drugs... and your bullies. You can all leave me alone!"

Demon Lynn shrank some more. Ten feet tall.

Rhian scrunched her face as she pointed to Aaron slumped against the curve of the wall.

"And you can leave him alone, too! Upset because like me, he learned who you are?" Then she growled as she pulled at the hair above her temples. "I don't care how much you hurt me out there. You're in my world now. Mine! So go ahead." Her arms slung low, and she stared Lynn down. Her fingers twitched from her palms and directed Lynn toward her. "Try it."

The sum of all her problems shrank some more within the pit until both Rhian and Lynn were at eye level with each other. A stare-down.

"I'm stronger than you, Lynn," Rhian smiled. She stared upon her abuser and proved Aaron right about the strength she held within her. A controlled breath in and a stretched one out.

"You are not... welcome... here!"

The once gigantic captor of Rhian's, the cause of all her pain and the reason she became trapped, exploded into a fit of sparks and ash upon Rhian's final words. It was a hell of a display. Like a single celebratory firework in the middle of the night, it lit up the entire room then settled into a peaceful dim blanket as the light of the pool disappeared with the fire.

Greeted with a welcome swarm of relief, Rhian held her hand to her chest.

"Aaron!" she gasped.

Her toes tapped in rhythm on the floor with every fluttered step she took. "Oh, thank God!" He was okay, battered and bruised, but okay.

She slapped him. A sharp flick of the right hand that met flush with his dirty bloodied cheek. "Are you crazy?" she shouted. As angry as she was, her hand still wiped the blood that leaked from his head into his left eye.

Aaron laughed with a splutter. "Maybe… got your attention though, didn't it? Huh?"

Rhian was lost. "Wait… you did that on purpose? I watched you… you waited for it."

"I never saved anybody," he said. "Every single part of you I've met… they had it in them all along. All it ever took was a little… encouragement." He looked down to his own beaten body, then to the emptied pit. "Point and case."

"You're a dick," Rhian laughed. She hugged the slumped man, tight. It hurt him more than he ever let on, but the pain was worth feeling her body against his again.

Aaron grabbed the hand that once wiped the blood from his eye and held it. "I guess Ember was right," he said.

Rhian pushed out from the hug to look him in the eyes. Question marks may as well have been painted across the whites of hers.

"When I was in her world," he explained. "She joked that you can't let a little fire bring you down. Ring any bells?"

Rhian took a glance at the empty crater where the fire once thrashed away and smiled.

"Yeah. I guess she was right. But what does this mean now?"

Aaron sighed gently. "I think it means you're ready to talk about all of this, properly now." He took a moment. "I know none of this will magically go away, that's not how it works, but I think it's a big step on a long road. I'll be right there beside you if you need it. You know I will."

Rhian agreed. He was right. She was still in a struggle with everything she'd come up against. It was like she'd watched a life that wasn't hers, only to find it actually *was* hers all along. It twisted her in new ways, but in the know of her old memories, she could open up and talk about what the others would actively choose to avoid. That was as good a start as any.

"Wise-ass," she joked.

"Yep," said Aaron. "That's Ember for you. Anyway… can we… leave? No offence but home sounds pretty good right now."

Rhian scanned the room that once held her hostage. The walls, the cage, the pit, and the stairs. She wouldn't miss any of it. But she did miss home, and she missed Aaron's voice.

"Yeah," she smiled. "Let's go home."

# 18
## RETURN TRIP

Aaron looked around. "Wait a minute."

There were no sirens and there was no fire. No neighbours who stuck their beaks where they didn't belong. Everything was silent and calm as he and Rhian huddled out of the door above the stairs of the pit.

"What's the matter," asked Rhian.

Aaron shook his head. He had to take another scan. "Wasn't like this when I left here."

No sign of any fire, the bungalow looked as it normally would with its overgrown gardens and scuffed door. Everything was vastly different, even the atmosphere.

"Nothing… I - Nothing." Not that he knew of, anyway.

Through their curiosity of things that may have changed, Aaron and Rhian reversed the trip Aaron had once taken. And it all started through the door of the bungalow that sat ahead of them. They followed it from the entrance, all the way up the flights of stairs that beckoned them, and as expected, it wasn't without its differences.

From step one, Rhian immediately sensed something was off. It stuck out to her like headlights on a dark road.

The bottom floor, once home to a memory of Rhian being beaten in the kitchen, was now altered. She watched by with tearful eyes as instead, Aaron was strewn on the floor ahead of a young Rhian. He took kicks and punches to the face and chest from Grant, Lynn's partner, while his topmost arm reached behind him and shielded the child from the onslaught.

Rhian turned her head to Aaron with a mere gentle twist of her neck. Her eyes moved from the ribs he held, to his cut lip, to the swollen eye he entered the pit with. He was fixed on the memory of himself that played in front of him. A smile on his face. No regrets.

As Rhian wondered what lay ahead, they took a right turn and ascended the next steps.

They entered into a diner. One Aaron remembered well.

The music and the smell. The nostalgic feel of the nineties. It was different, again. There was no Lynn and no Graham sat at the centre. Just a young Rhian as past Aaron stood over her in the booth by the window.

Rhian sank her head to the side and lapped her lips as she watched her partner feed her younger self a blue-iced muffin. Even then, she could almost taste how delicious it was. Those blueberry muffins were the best in the region.

Young Rhian looked so thankful to be eating. Of course, because she was. Before Aaron passed her that cake, she'd not eaten in a day. Rhian herself couldn't find the words she wanted to speak as she heard Aaron wish her young self a happy birthday as he walked off to the other side of the diner.

"Come on," ushered Aaron, and he and Rhian exited the door which led them up the next set of steps. At the top, they entered the living room of the bungalow they'd both seen too much of. Lynn was smoking and drinking, her usual day to day activities.

Rhian pulled on the sleeve of Aaron's t-shirt as they walked past the disgusting woman. Rhian held an extended finger to her pursed lips, and her free hand cupped behind her ear.

There was no sound of the distressed child that would scream in the background. Rhian knew that every time Lynn was in this state, it was after she'd served Rhian the abuse that would go on to give her nightmares. She'd been forced the memories so many times now, it was hard to forget it. But nothing but near-silence. The only noise came from the sloppy and rasped breaths that spat their way out of Lynn. That floor was about done, and Rhian eagerly pulled Aaron to the next appearance of stairs, and up they climbed, right into the next room.

Stars danced in the blacks of her eyes as Rhian stood by and watched with bundles of love.

Aaron was perched on the edge of her childhood bed, as he handed her younger self three pink bears. Bears she recognized.

"Here, these will protect you," he said. Then he wiped a tear from her eye and rested his hand on the back of the child's head.

Rhian couldn't stop herself but angle into a lean against Aaron's shoulder as they watched him calm the young girl. But as much as she could have watched it all day, they still had one more flight of stairs to climb. Up, and into the swirling abyss of black that had stumped Aaron. Even Rhian took a second look as she noted the ring of clouds that countered the centric motion. She thought the sparks a 'pretty addition,' though. Aaron agreed as they stepped through it, passed through the small room it sat in and opened the imposing steel door. Much like Ma'am's, Aaron forgot just how much it weighed.

On the other side, as they appeared from it, Rhian burst with her emotions and grabbed Aaron's shoulders before the door even shut fully. She pulled him in as tight as she could. Her arms wrapped around his body and the side of her face pushed firmly against his chest.

Aaron leaned his chin down an inch until it rested on the top of her head, and his arms too, stretched around her. Rhian just refused to let go, and her partner welcomed it. He'd missed it so vividly. The feel of her hugs, the smell of her hair, and how her breath would push through his shirt and warm his chest. He missed it all. It seemed forever since the last time he'd experienced it.

Into the padding of his breast, Rhian said, "You knew it wouldn't change anything, but you still helped her… me."

"I wish it did, I really do. But you know me, I just couldn't-"

"Just couldn't sit back and let it happen." Rhian knew exactly the man she loved.

Aaron smiled with his eyes. "Yeah. That."

Rhian's hug tightened, and she turned her head up to stare deep into eyes she could never lose the memory of. She kissed him. A long, overdue, perfectly earned kiss that said more than words ever could.

As her soft lips left his, she whispered, "I love you."

"And I love you," Aaron replied. "All… all eight of you."

She laughed for a moment. "Eight?" Did he know how to count? She began to list the names of the ones she was aware of and started with herself.

"There was another," he said. "I think less a personality and more… you. She called herself Rhiannon."

A name Rhian hadn't heard in years. At first, it made her wince as he remembered what that name endured as a child; why she changed it to Rhian, but then she asked, "What was she like?"

Aaron remembered their encounter. He didn't want Rhian to know how worn-down Rhiannon was. Nor did he want her to know how she'd begun to fade away as a result of it.

"Just like you," he said with a smile. He brushed her hair behind her ear. "Only better looking."

They shared a laugh as they left the heavy door of the tower. Aaron locked it tight, with a sharp twist of the key, and as he did, the key disintegrated into a cloud of black dust and floated away in the breeze.

*That's a little dramatic,* he thought.

He and Rhian took the steps down to the water after Rhian pointed out just how many there were… like

Aaron didn't already scale them, and they sat on the boat that rested in wait for them.

A boat that waded throughout a territory unlike one Aaron had already been through. The water was a deep ocean shade that reflected the pale blue brightness of the clear sky above. No clouds were in sight, but rather a midday sun that removed the shivers from the boat passengers and encouraged the blossom of flowers that blessed the scenery with a splash of colour and decoration it sorely missed.

The grass that surrounded the dock was neatly cut and a much healthier, young shade of green. As Aaron got off the boat, he couldn't help but notice how little effort it now took to walk on, and the lack of crunches under every step he took. The question that circled his mind, was that of how so much had changed in the short time since he last saw it.

After five minutes where they took in the breath-taking views and listened to the sound of nothing but a gentle breeze, they moved inside the building where Aaron told Rhian he'd entered the island from.

The building that was home to almost every door he'd opened, only Aaron didn't recognise anymore. Carpets lined the floors in a comfortable, silk grey. The walls were painted over in a clean white that brightened it, and the bars were removed from the windows. Instead, the windows were perched open, and they let the summer breeze flirt with them. It felt dream-like and welcoming. If it were a person, it would have invited them in with a platter of food and a glass of orange squash.

Around the corner, where he entered, Aaron counted forty-one steps and there it was as he turned the corner right. A door, brown in colour. A golden handle and letterbox that shimmered in the light. A boastful ornament right in the middle, of the same gold.

NO.27

The door of their home. There was no way to mistake it, the way out was right there in front of them. Finally, on proud display.

Aaron took one last look around him. Thankful for the lessons he'd learned and the people he'd met. Fond of it all and yet glad to be finished. He'd miss it, he really would, no matter how much he also was glad to leave.

"I'll follow you right out," Rhian said as she lingered a few feet behind him. "I just want to do one thing before I leave."

# 19

## WELCOME BACK

The flash of white light that blinded him was something Aaron never really got used to, but he soon managed to open his eyes. Something about the light on the return just… stuck around for much longer than the times before. It felt like he'd veered from a forever darkness and head-on into the face of the sun without so much as a pair of sunglasses.

Groggy, and a little dazed, he needed a minute. Everything felt strange.

"Mr Haze?" a voice called. Aaron recognised it.

"Mr Haze, sir?" Oswald repeated. "Damn it, stupid machine!" He thumped twice, hard on the side of the odd-looking device as it hissed and clunked away on the floor.

Among the mutters, moans, and grumbles, Aaron finally came too. The living room around him became clear, so much so he could see the swirling pattern in the plaster of the ceiling he looked upon. He sat up and pressed his hands against his face, chest, then legs, careful to mind the pipe that hung from his nose. He could feel them all. He was back in his white jumper, cleaner than ever. *Thank God for that.* Evident to him, he was *back*.

"Oswald?" The pipes in his nose messed with his voice. It sounded like he'd contracted a cold.

"Yes. Right here. Something's clearly not working as intended, I'll be right with you."

"Oswald!"

The aged man spun his neck round to face Aaron in an instant. He could have broken it with a move so fast. Impressive, given how slow he'd previously shown himself to be.

Aaron smiled at him. "It worked, relax."

Oswald shrugged away the lie. He wasn't happy. "Impossible. You've been tossing and turning for all of three minutes." Aaron's smile inverted faster than he could blink. "Th- Three minutes? I was in there for what felt like a week! Oswald, how-"

Aaron noticed the open box of biscuits on the coffee table above him, crumbs littered all over the surface. Some even made it to the floor. Aaron tutted.

"Did you help yourself to my biscuits?"

Oswald muttered something, then cleared his throat. A quick search for the answer... ah!

"It's hungry work, Mr Haze."

"Three... minutes, Oswald. Three minutes."

Two different tones left the doctor as he laughed his guilt away. His cheeks changed to a lovely rosy colour; they got warm pretty quick. He observed that Rhian hadn't woken yet, and his eyes questioned Aaron.

"She'll be awake soon," Aaron said. "She just wanted to do something."

"And you *let* her?"

The flexible pipe tickled Aaron's entire nervous system as he pulled it from his nose. A longer pull than he figured it'd take. "I don't own her, you know."

He flung the translucent pipe to the floor with a shudder whilst his system shook it off. Okay... no, it needed a second shudder. One wasn't enough. It was uncomfortable, to say the least.

The clock he turned to confirmed what Oswald had said. It was barely five-past-ten. Three minutes sounded about right.

He stood, stretched his legs, and yawned. Anxious to see Rhian return, he stood in wait as he watched her. It felt different as he did. He *knew* she was just moments from waking. The last time he stood in the same position, he almost pulled his own hair out with worry. That felt like forever ago, now.

Just as Oswald passed him a glass of water that he'd prepared for himself, Rhian began to stir.

Oswald rushed to her but was stopped by the hand of the man who towered above him. "Give her a minute, please. She's been through it."

"Right you are, I'll start loading up the van," the doctor winked with a tight smile. Aaron shared an appreciative nod with him. He wasn't so bad, Oswald. Aaron was still in one piece. He'd consider that a win for the doctor.

It took twenty-one minutes from when Rhian woke to when she found the strength to walk around. Finally in control of her own body once again. Well, nineteen of them were occupied by Rhian's desperate attempt to pull the pipes from her nose and poke fun at the 'alien' machine she was connected to. Aaron knew… he'd counted every single minute. She'd taken the time to swap the blanket that wrapped her legs in favour of some grey tracksuit trousers from the basket in the kitchen.

The crumbs that had spilt from the table onto the floor, ruffled her feathers a bit, too. All she had to do was stare at the doctor and point to the table. To Aaron's amusement, it wasn't long before it had been cleaned up by the apologetic old man.

Oswald had upwards of a million questions once he'd cleaned his mess and packed his 'souvenir' miracle machine into his van. But first, Aaron had one for him.

As the doctor sat upon the corner of the coffee table, invested in Rhian and her condition, Aaron asked, "So, three minutes, right? Why did it feel like days? Like… I don't know, a week?"

"Good question," said Rhian. A wide stretch saw her arms crack at the elbows. It felt nice. "Because I was stuck in this loop of memories that seemed to last hours… but it felt like I was sat inside that cage for months."

Oswald clapped his bony hands and gasped in excitement. "The dream state of mind. It all makes sense." His hands rubbed together; another clap felt like too much. It didn't take him long to realise he hadn't properly answered their questions.

"Sorry. When we wake from a dream, we remember… sometimes the duration of said dream, right?

"Let's suppose you dreamt of a weekend away in the Alps. You'd feel that entire weekend, but maybe you slept for six hours.

"Or maybe you dreamt of an event that lasted an hour, but you slept for eight… it's wonderful! Confusing, but wonderful."

The blank stares that faced him began to understand him more, even if it was in small drips.

"People tend to forget the mind is most active when we sleep, even me. The mind has no concept of exterior time when it's serving you internally."

"Okay…" Rhian wasn't impressed. She understood, but she didn't want to talk about it with a stranger. "I should call Doctor Perkins about this. He'd want to know what happened."

She grabbed her phone from the table and Aaron sunk his head into his hands.

"Shit," he said, internally. He moved his hands to the phone in her hand and gently lowered it, about to tell her something. Something that *should* have only come from him.

"Oh dear," said Oswald. "That's the poor fellow who passed away is it not?"

Aaron's teeth gritted at the same time his eyes jammed shut. "Yeah," he whispered through his teeth. It prompted a dark moment of silence from Rhian made him kick himself.

"I'm so sorry. I didn't get a chance to tell you. I rang for him first… the lady said he'd been gone a few months," Aaron said. "Everything that was going on I just-"

"It's okay." Rhian put the phone down and reached for Aaron's arm. "I guess it does explain the weird little guy," she said. Her eyes pointed right at the doctor as she aimed her insult.

Oswald jerked his head back and scrunched his nose. Rhian smiled at him. She didn't realise how loud she'd spoken.

They talked for two hours, the three. A clean-cut and thorough explanation of what the couple had endured in their time on the island. A tour, as it were, of its many worlds and features, and what Rhian had braved.

By the end, Oswald couldn't be happier to ask if he could keep Rhian on as a patient. Not able to turn to Felix anymore, she figured she'd give 'the weird little guy,' a chance.

He'd done his final inspection. After all, he wasn't leaving if there was any chance his new patient would veer off again. He was happy to leave them in peace. He even refused any payment Aaron offered him for his time.

"No, please," Oswald insisted. "I've learned so much from you interesting people. I'll put this one down as a lesson."

Aaron shook his hand. "Thanks, Oswald. For everything." The man did more than prove himself. He'd kept his word; Aaron had found and brought Rhian home.

"A pleasure, Mr Haze," he bowed.

Oswald drove off into the sunrise in his van which had seen much better days. The pops and squeaks it made as it revved along made Aaron chuckle a little as he closed the door.

He sat by Rhian in the living room, and he held her. He held her for real, for as long as he could, because he could once more.

"You," he said. "You're a pain in my arse, but I love you."

"I know." She shifted her head and tilted to him. "I took a little trip to that Rhiannon you spoke about. She told me everything you did."

"You saw her?"

"I did. I wish I could see how you affected them all. Sounds like you were busy."

Aaron laughed. "Just a bit."

He held memories now, of an entire world that nobody other than the woman sat beside him could share with him. Memories he hoped he would never, ever forget. Ones that connected them on a deeper level than any on the outside ever could.

"She really was beautiful," said Rhian.

Her phone caught her attention through the corner of her eye as she sunk into Aaron's hold. She lingered on it for a moment until something clicked. It widened her eyes when she gasped.

"I better call Bernice. She's going to have a meltdown over this one."

Aaron sucked the air through his teeth. "Yeah… good luck with that one," he laughed. "Tell her I said hey."

As she left the room in a hurry, phone in hand, Rhian turned to the man she left on the couch. "Every time I told you I was fine…" She looked down to the floor, for just a second. "I should have admitted I wasn't. Maybe things would have been different."

A fond look met her back.

"Maybe," said Aaron. "But then I wouldn't have met them all. I'm… happy I did. Sounds weird, considering… but I wouldn't take it back." He shrugged, then added, "Also, it might have helped you a bit." Rhian smiled. This time the gap between her lips showed the glow of her pristine white teeth in full. Something about the whole turn of events put a bounce in her step that she missed before. To look at her you could see how much more *her* she felt, and how much more her she *was*. Maybe the knowledge of her old memories, mixed with all the ones she'd gained over her time with Aaron and Bernice, made her realise just much power she really possessed.

In a way, it was odd that she looked forward to her call with Bernice, but, to her, it felt like they hadn't spoken in months, and as she floated to the kitchen as if she were carried by the wind, Aaron stood ahead of the television cabinet in the living room. He reached into the drawer and pulled out a plain brown box, opened it and pulled out a smaller, black box, lined in silk. He opened that, too.

The glint of the diamond-set silver ring that stared back, reflected on his face like a disco ball as the morning sun shone through the windows and bounced off of its beauty. He smiled wider than he ever had and shut the case. Its hinge snapped shut. Their lives were about to change, just a little bit more.

Needless to say, Rhian would never look at Aaron the same way again. She'd go on to remember everything he did for her. Everything he put himself through, and did, for *them*. All of them.

She was Rhian. She was Ember, Dolly, Ma'am, Littlefoot, Stephanie, Whisper, and Rhiannon. Whichever she went by, one thing remained: She was loved with no boundaries and no question. No motives and no strings.

Love. Exactly like she deserved.

Tormented as she was, she was never alone. She never will be, for of her, there are seven, and of those who love her, the numbers would continue to grow.

# EPILOGUE

The pit at the bottom of the lanky tower lay silent. Not a single shift of stone could be heard. Timid and gentle. Deservedly alone. A vast difference from the life it had known. It was a brief glimpse into the future it would now be burdened with.

Ember sat across from her coveted fall of lava. Her leather jacket was strewn underneath her, casual and relaxed. She whistled Ember to Inferno into the abyss. Happy, and rested. Aaron had done what she knew he could, what she told him he could.

Ma'am stood over her table. Rather than read a map, she'd flipped it blank side up and drawn her own. A sly

smile cemented into her washed face. She was ready for
whatever came next, only this time, nothing was written.
Her story was her own to choose, and the cluster of
options at her disposal lit her up.

Her three companions, the strong female bears,
watched by as Ma'am plotted their next objective. Their
masks were no longer needed; they felt it unnecessary to
hide who they were. Why wouldn't they? They were
accepted by an outsider-turned-ally they once held at
gunpoint, after all.

In their world of zombies, lasers and gunships, the
possibilities were now endless.

Littlefoot sat in her beautiful pink tent beneath the
crevice in the garden rockery. She read a book to her
three bears about a man from another world who'd
shown a vulnerable princess her true strength.

She lit a smile as the blue illumination of the moon
leaked into her sanctuary. Far from that which scared
her, Littlefoot had never felt such peace of mind in as
long as she could remember.

Whisper lay on the couch in the corner of her dark room.
She wore the mask Aaron had given her. But she wasn't
cowered or scared. She lay, legs kicked out onto the
opposite arm, more comfortable than she'd ever been
before.

A gentle hum as she sunk into the padding of the cushions. Into a sleep, she fell. One through comfort and silence, not fought against by the voices that once bombarded her space.

Rhiannon sat on the bench by the pool. Drained of the blood it once held, though the six counted lines remained in the sill that ran the outside. A crack gaped down it, where its contents once gushed out. Scarred for eternity.

On the bench, Rhiannon stared into the ceiling as light poured through gaps in the tiles. She was waiting for something.

The floating scatter of disintegration that reached out from her left side began to pull back to her face until it was whole again. The dark, rotted tint disappeared. The cracks in her skin, the same. Until she looked like the spitting image of Rhian, only in a gentle, heaven-like luminescence.

"Thank you," she whispered in echo as the enormous weight she held, lifted. She faded away like the clouds that once lines the island, and the room emptied.

Rhiannon wasn't needed anymore. Rhian had accepted who she was. She had accepted Rhiannon as part of her.

Rhian sat on the couch with Aaron as they read a book. Happy. Nothing to hide, and not as scared. She closed the book she held, and the sparkle of the diamond ring she wore, danced along the walls.

She placed the book neatly on the coffee table, kicked up her feet and cuddled into her fiancé.

A lease of new life had dawned for Rhian, and though it may not be perfect, and her problems hadn't miraculously vanished, she was more open to exploring every part of herself, and the others who called her home.

It all started with a well-deserved break, and... a period piece drama she'd finally convinced Aaron to watch.

# SHE TORMENTED

For Mum.
I love you, endless.
I miss you, forever.
This was for you. Without you, I'd be nothing.